Works by J.R.R. Tolkien

THE HOBBIT

LEAF BY NIGGLE

ON FAIRY-STORIES

FARMER GILES OF HAM

THE HOMECOMING OF BEORHTNOTH

THE LORD OF THE RINGS

THE ADVENTURES OF TOM BOMBADIL

THE ROAD GOES EVER ON (WITH DONALD SWANN)

SMITH OF WOOTTON MAJOR

Works published posthumously

SIR GAWAIN AND THE GREEN KNIGHT, PEARL AND SIR ORFEO*

THE FATHER CHRISTMAS LETTERS

THE SILMARILLION*

PICTURES BY J.R.R. TOLKIEN*

UNFINISHED TALES*

THE LETTERS OF J.R.R. TOLKIEN*

FINN AND HENGEST

MR BLISS

THE MONSTERS AND THE CRITICS & OTHER ESSAYS*

ROVERANDOM

THE CHILDREN OF HÚRIN*

THE LEGEND OF SIGURD AND GUDRÚN*

THE FALL OF ARTHUR*

BEOWULF: A TRANSLATION AND COMMENTARY*

The History of Middle-earth – by Christopher Tolkien

I THE BOOK OF LOST TALES, PART ONE

II THE BOOK OF LOST TALES, PART TWO

III THE LAYS OF BELERIAND

IV THE SHAPING OF MIDDLE-EARTH

V THE LOST ROAD AND OTHER WRITINGS

VI THE RETURN OF THE SHADOW

VII THE TREASON OF ISENGARD

VIII THE WAR OF THE RING

IX SAURON DEFEATED

X MORGOTH'S RING

XI THE WAR OF THE JEWELS

XII THE PEOPLES OF MIDDLE-EARTH

* Edited by Christopher Tolkien

THE STORY OF
KULLERVO

THE STORY OF KULLERVO

BY

J.R.R. Tolkien

Edited by Verlyn Flieger

HOUGHTON MIFFLIN HARCOURT

BOSTON   NEW YORK

2016

CONTENTS

LIST OF PLATES

FOREWORD

Kullervo son of Kalervo is, perhaps, the least ingratiating of Tolkien's heroes: uncouth, moody, bad-tempered and vengeful, as well as physically unattractive. Yet those traits add realism to his character, making him perversely appealing in spite of, or perhaps because of, them. I welcome the chance to introduce this complex character to a wider readership than heretofore. I am also grateful for the opportunity to refine my first transcription of the manuscript, restore inadvertent omissions, emend conjectural readings, and correct typos that found their way into print. The present text is, I hope, an improved representation of what Tolkien intended.

Since the story's initial appearance, further work has been done on its role in the development of Tolkien's early proto-language, Qenya. John Garth and Andrew Higgins have explored the names of both people and places in the surviving drafts and related them to his language invention, John in his article 'The road from adaptation to invention' (*Tolkien Studies* Vol. XI, pp. 1–44), and Andrew in Chapter Two of his ground-breaking PhD dissertation on

Tolkien's early languages, 'The Genesis of J.R.R. Tolkien's Mythology' (Cardiff Metropolitan University, 2015). Their work adds to our knowledge of Tolkien's early efforts, and enriches our understanding of his legendarium as a whole.

The materials here published, J.R.R. Tolkien's unfinished early work *The Story of Kullervo* and the two drafts of his Oxford University talk on its source 'On "The Kalevala"', first appeared in *Tolkien Studies* Volume VII in 2010, and I am grateful for the permission of the Tolkien Estate to reprint them here. My Notes and Comments are reprinted with the permission of West Virginia University Press. My essay, 'Tolkien, *Kalevala*, and "The Story of Kullervo"', is reprinted with the permission of Kent State University Press.

Thanks for the present volume go to several people, without whom it would never have come to be. First of all to Cathleen Blackburn, to whom I first proposed that *The Story of Kullervo* needed to reach a larger audience than that of a scholarly journal. I am grateful to Cathleen for ushering the project through the permissions process of the Tolkien Estate and its publisher, HarperCollins. I am grateful to both the Estate and HarperCollins for agreeing with me that re-publication as a stand-alone was what Tolkien's *Kullervo* merited. Thanks also to Chris Smith, Editorial Director at HarperCollins in charge of matters Tolkienian, for his help, advice, and encouragement in bringing Tolkien's *The Story of Kullervo* to the wider audience it deserves. For help and advice in preparing the story and essays, thanks go to Catherine Parker, Carl Hostetter, Petri Tikka and Rob Wakeman.

INTRODUCTION

The Story of Kullervo needs to be looked at from several angles if we are to appreciate fully its place in J.R.R. Tolkien's body of work. It is not only Tolkien's earliest short story, but also his earliest attempt to write tragedy, as well as his earliest prose venture into myth-making, and is thus a general precursor to his entire fictional canon. In a narrower focus it is a seminal source for what has come to be called his 'mythology for England', the 'Silmarillion'. His retelling of the saga of hapless Kullervo is the raw material from which he developed one of his most powerful stories, that of the Children of Húrin. More specifically still, the character of Kullervo was the germ of Tolkien's mythology's most – some would say its only – tragic hero, Túrin Turambar.

It has long been known from Tolkien's letters that his discovery as a schoolboy of *Kalevala* or 'Land of Heroes', a then recently-published collection of the songs or *runos* of unlettered peasants in Finland's rural countryside, had a powerful impact on his imagination and was one of the earliest influences on his invented legendarium. In his 1951 letter describing his mythology to the publisher Milton Waldman Tolkien voiced the concern he had always had for the mythological 'poverty' of his own country. It was lacking in his eyes, 'stories of its own' comparable to the myths of other countries. There was, he wrote, 'Greek, and Celtic, and Romance, Germanic, Scandinavian', and (singled out for special mention) 'Finnish,' which he said, 'greatly affected' him (*The Letters of J.R.R. Tolkien*, p. 144, hereafter *Letters*). Affect him it most certainly did, his engagement with it nearly ruining his Honour Moderations examinations of 1913, as he confessed to his son Christopher in 1944 (*Letters*, p. 87), and 'set[ting] the rocket off in story', as he wrote to W.H. Auden in 1955 (*Letters*, pp. 214–15).

At the time Tolkien was working on his story its source, the Finnish *Kalevala*, was a latecomer to the existing corpus of world mythologies. Unlike the myths of longer literary provenance such as the Greek and Roman, or the Celtic or Germanic, the songs of *Kalevala* were gathered and published only in the mid-19th century by a professional physician and amateur folklorist, Elias Lönnrot. So different in tone were these songs from the rest of the European myth corpus that they brought about a re-evaluation of the meaning of such terms as *epic* and *myth*.* Difference and

---

* They also raised questions about the role of the collector in selecting, editing, and presenting what is collected, leading to the accusation, specific to *Kalevala*, of 'folklore or fakelore'; but that is a subject for a different discussion. When Tolkien was first reading *Kalevala* he and others took it at face value.

re-evaluation notwithstanding, the publication of *Kalevala*
had a profound effect on the Finns, who had lived under
foreign rule for centuries – as part of Sweden from the
13th century to 1809, and from then to 1917 as a sub-set
of Russia to which large parts of Finnish territory were
ceded by Sweden. The discovery of an indigenous Finnish
mythology, coming as it did at a time when myth was
becoming associated with nationalism, gave the Finns a
sense of cultural independence and a national identity,
and made Lönnrot a national hero. *Kalevala* energized
a burgeoning Finnish nationalism and was influential in
Finland's declaration of independence from Russia in 1917.
It seems more than possible that *Kalevala*'s impact on the
Finns as 'a mythology for Finland' might have made as
deep an impression on Tolkien as the songs themselves,
and played a major part in his expressed desire to create
his so-called 'mythology for England', though what he
actually described was a mythology that he could 'dedicate'
to England (*Letters,* p. 144). The fact that he would go on
to absorb his Kullervo into the character of his own mythology's Túrin Turambar is evidence of *Kalevala*'s continuing
influence on his creativity.

Tolkien had first read *Kalevala* in the 1907 English
translation of W.F. Kirby while a student at King Edward's
School in Birmingham in 1911. He thought Kirby's translation unsatisfactory, but found the material itself to be
like 'an amazing wine' (*Letters,* p. 214). Both his story and
the accompanying two drafts of his college talk, 'On "The
Kalevala"', give evidence of Tolkien's enthusiastic desire to

communicate the taste of this new wine, its fresh and pagan flavour and the 'delicious exaggerations' of what were to him 'wild ... uncivilized and primitive tales'. These uncivilized and primitive tales so captured his imagination that when he went up to Oxford in the fall of 1911, he borrowed C.N.E. Eliot's *Finnish Grammar* from the Exeter College Library in an attempt to teach himself enough Finnish to read the original. He was largely unsuccessful, and ruefully confessed he had been 'repulsed with heavy losses'.

Tolkien was particularly taken by the character he called 'Kullervo the hapless' (*Letters*, p. 214), *Kalevala*'s closest approximation of a tragic hero. So taken, indeed, was he that in his final year as an Oxford undergraduate he wrote to his fiancée Edith Bratt, some time in October of 1914, that he was 'trying to turn one of the stories – which is really a very great story and most tragic – into a short story ... with chunks of poetry in between' (*Letters*, p. 7). This was 'The Story of Kullervo', the bulk of which was produced, as nearly as can be ascertained, some time during the years 1912–14 (ibid., 214) and almost certainly before his war service intervened and he was sent to France in 1916. The dating is problematic. Tolkien himself placed it as early as 1912; scholars Wayne Hammond and Christina Scull prefer 1914; and John Garth sets it at late 1914. The manuscript title page (Plate 1) carries a date in parentheses '(1916)' in Christopher Tolkien's hand, but as this is written on the verso of an appreciation on the occasion of Tolkien's honorary Doctorate from the National University of Ireland in 1954, the 1916 date is retrospective by almost forty years. The 1916 date is further called into question by a notation written below it in pencil: 'HC [Humphrey Carpenter] says 1914.' This comment would have been made during or after the time when Carpenter was at work on his biography of Tolkien, published in 1977.

Any work's time of composition is often difficult to determine with precision, since most creative activity develops over an extended period from first idea to final version and can be started, stopped, revised and re-revised along the way. Without more manuscript evidence than we now possess, it is impossible to pinpoint the time of Tolkien's work on 'Kullervo' from inspiration to cessation any more narrowly than during the years 1912–1916. What is fairly certain is that he did not begin work on the story before he read *Kalevala* in 1911, and may not have done further work on it after his posting to France in June of 1916. From Tolkien's comment in the letter to Edith, it seems to have been the story's tragic qualities as much as its mythic qualities that 'set the rocket off in story', and so powerfully attracted him that he felt the need to re-tell it.

Aside from its palpable influence on the story of Túrin Turambar, however, *The Story of Kullervo* is notable also for the ways in which it prefigures the narrative styles of Tolkien's future corpus. It presages without precisely fitting a number of the genres or categories or forms – short story, tragedy, myth-retelling, verse, prose – in which he later wrote. It is at once a short story, a tragedy, a myth, a blend of prose and poetry, yet – hardly surprising in so early a work – all of these in embryo, none fully realized. Thus in all these areas it stands a little to one side of the rest of the canon. As a short story it invites comparison with his later short stories, *Roverandom*, *Leaf By Niggle*, *Farmer Giles of Ham*, and *Smith of Wootton Major*; as a myth re-telling it belongs with his *Legend of Sigurd and Gudrún* and *The Fall of Arthur*; in its mix of prose and poetry it recalls a similar mixture in Tolkien's masterwork, *The Lord of the Rings*. Stylistically, too, there is ground for comparison, for the 'chunks of poetry' not infrequently segue into a rhythmic prose that evokes the poetry-prose mix of the speech of Tom Bombadil.

The comparisons end there, however, for in other aspects *The Story of Kullervo* has little in common with most of the above works. Only *The Legend of Sigurd and Gudrún* conveys the pagan atmosphere that is the essence of *Kullervo*, and *The Fall of Arthur* its sense of ineluctable doom. *Roverandom*, although it has, as recently pointed out, distinct similarities to the mythic Irish *imramma* or voyage stories,* was in its genesis and essentially remains a tale for children. *Leaf By Niggle*, although it is set in vaguely modern times and in a place that, while never identified, is pretty clearly Tolkien's own England, is a parable about the journey of the soul, and by far the most allegorical of all Tolkien's works. *Farmer Giles of Ham* is a playfully satiric pseudo-folktale with a number of scholarly

---

* See Kris Swank's article 'The Irish Otherworld Voyage of *Roverandom*' in *Tolkien Studies* Volume XII, planned for publication in 2015.

inside jokes and topical references to Tolkien's Oxford. *Smith of Wootton Major* is pure fairy tale, the most artistically consistent of all his shorter works. In contrast to all of these, *The Story of Kullervo* – emphatically not for children, neither playful nor satiric, not allegorical, and with little of the faërie quality Tolkien found essential for fairy stories – is relentlessly dark, a foreboding and tragic tale of blood feud, murder, child abuse, revenge, incest and suicide, so different in tone and content from his other short fiction as to be almost a separate category.

As a tragedy, *The Story of Kullervo* conforms in large measure to the Aristotelian specifics for tragedy: *catastrophe*, or change of fortune; *peripeteia*, or reversal, in which a character inadvertently produces an effect opposite to what is intended; and *anagnoresis*, or recognition, in which a character moves from ignorance to self-knowledge. The classic example is Oedipus, whose drama Sophocles situated within quasi-historical time and place – Thebes in the 4th century BC. Tolkien's fictive Middle-earth examples are Túrin Turambar, who is closely modelled on Kullervo, and his least likely tragic hero Frodo Baggins, whose journey and emotional trajectory from Bag End to Mount Doom take him through all of Aristotle's norms set within the larger context of the history of Middle-earth, as do those of Túrin. In contrast, *The Story of Kullervo* is largely ahistorical, creating its own self-contained world whose only time-period is 'when magic was yet new.'

As Tolkien's earliest effort to adapt an existing myth to his own purpose, *The Story of Kullervo* belongs with his two other, more mature such efforts, both conjecturally dated to the 1920s–30s. These are *The Legend of Sigurd and Gudrún*, his verse retelling of the Völsung story from the Icelandic *Poetic Edda*, and *The Fall of Arthur*, his synthesis and recasting into modern English alliterative verse of two Middle English Arthurian poems. Like his Arthur and Sigurd, Tolkien's Kullervo is the latest version of a mythic figure who has had many iterations. Aspects of Kullervo can be traced back to the early medieval Irish Amlodhi, to the Scandinavian Amlethus of Saxo Grammaticus's 12th-century *Gesta Danorum*, and to Shakespeare's more modern Renaissance Prince Hamlet. The sequence culminates in *Kalevala's* Kullervo, to which Tolkien is most directly indebted. And yet Tolkien's story does not quite fit with his later mythic adaptations either. First, both *Kalevala* and Tolkien's Kullervo are considerably less well-known than are Sigurd and Arthur. *The Story of Kullervo* will, for many readers who are acquainted with Sigurd and Arthur, be their first introduction to this unlikely hero. Thus Tolkien's version carries no baggage and is likely to be met with no preconceptions. Few, if any, of his readers will recognize Shakespeare's Prince Hamlet in Tolkien's Kullervo, though sharp eyes may see in Kullervo's ruthless and unscrupulous uncle Untamo the seed of Hamlet's ruthless and unscrupulous uncle, Claudius.

In terms of narrative form, Tolkien's 'Kullervo' falls somewhere between the short stories and the long poems in that it is cast in a mixture of prose and verse, interpolating long passages of poetry into a stylized prose narrative. Like his *Sigurd and Gudrún* it is a love story of doom with no reprieve for its human players, and like his *Fall of Arthur* it is a story of the intermixture of fate and human decision as the relentless determinants of human life. Also, like *The Fall of Arthur* but unlike *Sigurd and Gudrún*, it is unfinished, breaking off before the climactic final scenes, which remain only sketched in jotted outline and notes. Its unfinished state is also sadly typical of much of Tolkien's work; more of his 'Silmarillion' stories remained works in progress at the time of his death than were ever brought to completion in his lifetime. Aside from this negative qualification, *The Story of Kullervo* would deserve a place in the continuum of Tolkien's art for all of the above-cited reasons.

But the greatest importance of *The Story of Kullervo*, as noted above, is as the preliminary to one of the foundation narratives of his legendarium, *The Children of Húrin*, its central character being the clear precursor of that story's protagonist, Túrin Turambar. Tolkien also cited other models for Túrin, such as the Icelandic *Edda* from which he borrowed Túrin's dragon-slaying episode, and Sophocles's Oedipus, who is (as defined above), like Túrin, a tragic hero in search of his own identity. Nevertheless, it is no exaggeration to say that without *Kalevala* there would be no *Story of Kullervo*, and without *The Story of Kullervo* there would be no Túrin. Certainly without the story of Túrin Tolkien's invented mythology would lack much of its tragic power, as well as its most compelling narrative trajectory outside *The Lord of the Rings*. We can also recognize in 'Kullervo', though more distantly, a number of repeating motifs that run through Tolkien's fiction: the fatherless child, the supernatural helper, the charged relationship of uncle and nephew, and the cherished heirloom or talisman. Although these motifs are translated into new narrative circumstances and sometimes turned in quite different directions, they nevertheless form a continuum that stretches from *The Story of Kullervo*, his earliest serious fiction, to *Smith of Wootton Major*, the last of his stories published in his lifetime.

In the above-mentioned letter to Waldman Tolkien expressed his hope that his invented myth would leave scope for 'other minds and hands wielding paint and music and drama' (*Letters*, pp. 144–5). He might have been thinking of *Kalevala* here also, for his reference to paint and music and the scope for other hands may well be an allusion to the translations of *Kalevala* material into paint and music by other artists who found in it inspiration for their art. Two prominent examples are the classical composer Jan Sibelius and the painter Akseli Gallen-Kallela, two of the best-known Finnish artists of the late 19th and early 20th century. Sibelius mined *Kalevala* for his orchestral 'Lemminkainen' and 'Tapiola' suites and his longer 'Kullervo Suite' for orchestra and chorus, turning myths into music. Akseli Gallen-Kallela, Finland's foremost painter of the modern era, produced a series of scenes from *Kalevala* including four paintings illustrating key moments in the life of Kullervo. The popularity of this character, and his attraction for artists, suggests that he can be seen as a kind of folkloric embodiment of the violence and troubled irrationality of the equally troubled modern age. It does not take a great stretch of imagination to see Tolkien's Túrin Turambar, a product of the same war-torn age, in the same light as the same sort of hero.

The narrative trajectory of Tolkien's story follows closely *runos* 31–36 in *Kalevala*. These were titled in Kirby's translation, 'Untamo and Kullervo', 'Kullervo and the Wife of Ilmarinen', 'The Death of Ilmarinen's Wife', 'Kullervo and his Parents', 'Kullervo and his Sister', and 'The Death of Kullervo'. Although presented as separate poems, they comprise a coherent (if not always fully integrated) sequence telling the continuous story of a catastrophic quarrel between brothers, which leaves one brother dead and the other the murderous guardian of the dead brother's newborn son, Kullervo. Mistreated and abused by both his guardian and the guardian's wife, the boy survives an unhappy childhood including three attempts at his murder – by drowning, burning, and hanging – and ultimately exacts vengeance on both of them, but is himself subsequently destroyed by his discovery of his unwitting incest with a sister he did not recognize until too late. Tolkien's treatment deepens the story, prolonging suspense and adding both psychology and mystery, developing the characters while preserving and enhancing the pagan and primitive qualities that first attracted him to *Kalevala*.

The Story of Kullervo exists in a single manuscript, Bodleian Library MS Tolkien B 64/6. This is a legible but rough draft, with many crossings-out, marginal and above-the-line additions, corrections, and emendations. The text is written in pencil on both sides of thirteen numbered bi-fold foolscap folios. The main narrative breaks off abruptly halfway down the recto of folio 13, at a point about three-quarters of the way through the story. It is followed on the same page by notes and outlines for the remainder (Plates 4, 5), which fill the rest of the space and continue on to the top portion of the verso. There are in addition several loose sheets of variable size containing what are clearly preliminary plot outlines, jotted notes, lists of names (Plate 3), lists of rhyming words, and several drafts of one long verse passage of the story, 'Now in sooth a man I deem me'. If, as appears likely, MS Tolkien B 64/6 contains the earliest and (aside from the note pages) the only draft of the story, Tolkien's revisions on this manuscript must stand as his final ones.

I have left intact Tolkien's sometimes quirky usage and often convoluted syntax, in a few instances adding punctuation where necessary to clarify meaning. Square brackets enclose conjectural readings and words or word-elements missing from the manuscript but supplied for clarity. His use of diacritical marks over the vowel – chiefly macron but also occasionally breve and umlaut – is also inconsistent, attributable more to speed of composition than intentional omission. False starts, cancelled words and lines have been omitted, with four exceptions. In these instances, wavy brackets enclose phrases or sentences cancelled in the MS but here retained as of particular interest to the story. Three such cancelled passages give evidence of Tolkien's long preoccupation with the nature of magic and the supernatural. The first two occur in the opening sentence. These are: 1) 'of magic long ago'; 2) 'when magic was yet new'. A third, the long sentence beginning 'and to Kullervo he [Musti] gave three hairs ...' refers to Kullervo's supernatural helper, the dog Musti, and is also evidence of the story's engagement with magic. The fourth, which occurs later in the text is the possibly autobiographically-related, 'I was small and lost my mother ...'

I have preferred not to interrupt the text (and distract the reader) with note numbers, but a Notes and Commentary section follows the narrative proper, explaining terms and usage, citing references, and clarifying the relationship of Tolkien's story to its *Kalevala* source. This section also includes Tolkien's preliminary outline notes for the story, enabling the reader to track apparent changes and follow the path of Tolkien's imagination.

The present edition of Tolkien's story, together with the accompanying drafts of his essay 'On "The Kalevala"', makes available to scholars, critics and readers alike the 'very great' and 'most tragic' story about which Tolkien wrote to Edith in 1914, and which contributed so materially to his legendarium. It is to be hoped they will find it a worthwhile and valuable addition to his work.

A Note on Names

The story is a work in progress not only for its narrative incompletion but because Tolkien began by following the

Kalevala nomenclature, but in the course of composition changed to his own invented names and nicknames for all but the major characters, these being the murdered brother Kalervo, his son Kullervo, and the murderous brother/ uncle Untamo; and even for these he supplied a variety of non-*Kalevala* nicknames. His text is not always consistent, however, and he occasionally reverts to, or forgets to change, an earlier discarded name. His most notable name-change is from 'Ilmarinen', the name of the smith in *Kalevala*, to 'Āsemo' for the same figure in his own story. See the entry for Āsemo the smith in the Notes and Commentary for a longer discussion on the etymology of the name. Tolkien also experimented with alternative names for two characters, Kullervo's sister Wanōna and his dog Musti.

It has been pointed out to me by Carl Hostetter that some of the invented names in *The Story of Kullervo* echo or prefigure Tolkien's earliest known efforts at his proto-invented language, Qenya. Qenya-like names in the story include the god-names *Ilu*, *Ilukko* and *Ilwinti*, all strongly reminiscent of *Ilúvatar*, the godhead figure of the 'Silmaril-lion'. Kalervo's nickname *Kampa* appears in early Qenya as a name for one of Tolkien's earliest figures, Earendel, with the meaning 'Leaper'. The place-name variously given as *Kēme* or *Kĕmĕnūme*, in Tolkien's story glossed as 'The Great Land, Russia' (Plate 2), is in Qenya defined as 'earth, soil'. The place-name *Telea* (actual Karelja) evokes the Teleri of the 'Silmarillion', one of the three groups of elves to go to Valinor from Middle-earth. *Manalome*, *Manatomi*,

Manoini, words for 'sky, heaven', recall Qenya *Mana/Manwë*, chief of the Valar, the demi-gods of the 'Silmaril-lion'. Circumstantial evidence would appear to support a chronological relationship between the names in *The Story of Kullervo* and Tolkien's burgeoning Qenya, the earliest evidences for which are contained in the Qenya Lexicon.

For a more extended look at the development of Qenya the reader is referred to Tolkien's 'Qenyaqetsa: The Qenya Phonology and Lexicon,' apparently written in 1915–16 and published in *Parma Eldalamberon* XII, 1998.

VERLYN FLIEGER

The Story of Kullervo

The Story of Kullervo

Unfinished prose romance
with interspersed verse, based
on Kalevala Runo XXXI ff.

(1916).

Hesvari 1917

1. Manuscript title page written in Christopher Tolkien's
hand [MS Tolkien B 64/6 folio 1 recto].

2. First folio of the manuscript
[MS Tolkien B 64/6 folio 2 recto].

The Story of Kullervo
(Kalervonpoika)

In the days {of magic long ago} {when magic was yet new}, a swan nurtured her brood of cygnets by the banks of a smooth river in the reedy marshland of Sutse. One day as she was sailing among the sedge-fenced pools with her trail of younglings following, an eagle swooped from heaven and flying high bore off one of her children to Telea: on the second day a mighty hawk robbed her of yet another and bore it to Kemenūme. Now that nursling that was brought to Kemenūme waxed and became a trader and cometh not into this sad tale: but that one whom the hawk brought to Telea he it is whom men name Kalervō: while a third of the nurslings that remained behind men speak oft of him and name him Untamō the Evil, and a fell sorcerer and man of power did he become.

And Kalervo dwelt beside the rivers of fish and had thence much sport and good meat, and to him had his wife borne in years past both a son and a daughter and was even now again nigh to childbirth. And in those days did Kalervo's lands border on the confines of the dismal realm of his mighty brother Untamo; who coveted his pleasant river lands and its plentiful fish.

So coming he set nets in Kalervo's fish waters and robbed Kalervo of his angling and brought him great grief. And bitterness arose between the brothers, first that and at last open war. After a fight upon the river banks in which neither might overcome the other, Untamo returned to his grim homestead and sat in evil brooding, weaving (in his fingers) a design of wrath and vengeance.

He caused his mighty cattle to break into Kalervo's pastures and drive his sheep away and devour their fodder. Then Kalervo let forth his black hound Musti to devour them. Untamo then in ire mustered his men and gave them weapons; armed his henchmen and slave lads with axe and sword and marched to battle, even to ill strife against his very brother.

And the wife of Kalervoinen sitting nigh to the window of the homestead descried a scurry arising of the smoke army in the distance, and she spake to Kalervo saying, 'Husband, lo, an ill reek ariseth yonder: come hither to me. Is it smoke I see or but a thick[?] gloomy cloud that passeth swift: but now hovers on the borders of the cornfields just yonder by the new-made pathway?'

Then said Kalervo in heavy mood, 'Yonder, wife, is no reek of autumn smoke nor any passing gloom, but I fear me a cloud that goeth nowise swiftly nor before it has harmed my house and folk in evil storm.' Then there came into the view of both Untamo's assemblage and ahead could they see the numbers and their strength and their gay scarlet raiment. Steel shimmered there and at their belts were their swords hanging and in their hands their stout axes gleaming and neath their caps their ill faces lowering: for ever did Untamoinen gather to him cruel and worthless carles.

And Kalervo's men were out and about the farm lands so seizing axe and shield he rushed alone on his foes and was soon slain even in his own yard nigh to the cowbyre in the autumn-sun of his own fair harvest-tide by the weight of the numbers of foemen. Evilly Untamoinen wrought with his brother's body before his wife's eyes and foully entreated his folk and lands. His wild men slew all whom they found both man and beast, sparing only Kalervo's wife and her two children and sparing them thus only to bondage in his gloomy halls of Untola.

Bitterness then entered the heart of that mother, for Kalervo had she dearly loved and dear been to him and she dwelt in the halls of Untamo caring naught for anything in the sunlit world: and in due time bore amidst her sorrow Kalervo's babes: a man-child and a maid-child at one birth. Of great strength was the one and of great fairness the other even at birth and dear to one another from their first hours: but their mother's heart was dead within, nor did she reck aught of their goodliness nor did it gladden her grief or do better than recall the old days in their homestead of the smooth river and the fish waters among the reeds and the thought of the dead Kalervo their father, and she named the boy Kullervo, or 'wrath', and his daughter Wanōna, or 'weeping'. And Untamo spared the children for he thought they would wax to lusty servants and he could have them do his bidding and tend his body nor pay them the wages he paid the other uncouth carles. But for lack of their mother's care the children were reared in crooked fashion, for ill cradle rocking meted to infants by fosterers in thralldom: and bitterness do they suck from breasts of those that bore them not.

The strength of Kullervo unsoftened turned to untameable will that would forego naught of his desire and was resentful of all injury. And a wild lone-faring maiden did Wanōna grow, straying in the grim woods of Untola so soon as she could stand – and early was that, for wondrous were these children and but one generation from the men of magic. And Kullervo was like to her: an ill child he ever was to handle till came the day that in wrath he rent in pieces his swaddling clothes and kicked with his strength his linden cradle to splinters – but men said that it seemed he would prosper and make a man of might and Untamo was glad, for him thought he would have in Kullervo one day a warrior of strength and a henchman of great stoutness.

Nor did this seem unlike, for at the third month did Kullervo, not yet more than knee-high, stand up and spake in this wise on a sudden to his mother who was grieving still in her yet green anguish. 'O my mother, o my dearest why grievest thou thus?' And his mother spake unto him telling him the dastard tale of the Death of Kalervo in his own homestead and how all he had earned was ravished and slain by his brother Untamo and his underlings, and nought spared or saved but his great hound Musti who had returned from the fields to find his master slain and his mistress and her children in bondage, and had followed their exile steps to the blue woods round Untamo's halls where now he dwelt a wild life for fear of Untamo's henchmen and ever and anon slaughtered a sheep and often at the night could his baying be heard: and Untamo's underlings said it was the hound of Tuoni Lord of Death though it was not so.

All this she told him and gave him a great knife curious wrought that Kalervo had worn ever at his belt if he fared afield, a blade of marvellous keenness made in his dim days, and she had caught it from the wall in the hope to aid her dear one.

Thereat she returned to her grief and Kullervo cried aloud, 'By my father's knife when I am bigger and my body waxeth stronger then will I avenge his slaughter and atone for the tears of thee my mother who bore me.' And these words he never said again but that once, but that once did Untamo overhear. And for wrath and fear he trembled and said he will bring my race in ruin for Kalervo is reborn in him.

And therewith he devised all manner of evil for the boy (for so already did the babe appear, so sudden and so marvellous was his growth in form and strength) and only his twin sister the fair maid Wanōna (for so already did she appear, so great and wondrous was her growth in form and beauty) had compassion on him and was his companion in their wandering the blue woods: for their elder brother and sister (of which the tale told before), though they had been born in freedom and looked on their father's face, were more like unto thralls than those orphans born in bondage, and knuckled under to Untamo and did all his evil bidding nor in anything recked to comfort their mother who had nurtured them in the rich days by the river.

And wandering in the woods a year and a month after their father Kalervo was slain these two wild children fell in with Musti the Hound. Of Musti did Kullervo learn many things concerning his father and Untamo and of things darker and dimmer and farther back even perhaps before their magic days and even before men as yet had netted fish in Tuoni the marshland.

Now Musti was the wisest of hounds: nor do men say ever aught of where or when he was whelped but ever speak of him as a dog of fell might and strength and of great knowledge, and Musti had kinship and fellowship with the things of the wild, and knew the secret of the changing of skin and could appear as wolf or bear or as cattle great or small and could much other magic besides. And on the night of which it is told, the hound warned them of the evil of Untamo's mind and that he desired nothing so much as Kullervo's death {and to Kullervo he gave three hairs from his coat, and said, 'Kullervo Kalervanpoika, if ever you are in danger from Untamo take one of these and cry 'Musti O! Musti may thy magic aid me now', then wilt thou find a marvellous aid in thy distress.'}

And next day Untamo had Kullervo seized and crushed into a barrel and flung into the waters of a rushing torrent – that seemed like to be the waters of Tuoni the River of Death to the boy: but when they looked out upon the river three days after, he had freed himself from the barrel and was sitting upon the waves fishing with a rod of copper with a silken line for fish, and he ever remained from that day a mighty catcher of fish. Now this was the magic of Musti.

And again did Untamo seek Kullervo's destruction and sent his servants to the woodland where they gathered mighty birch trees and pine trees from which the pitch was oozing, pine trees with their thousand needles. And sledge-fuls of bark did they draw together, and great ash trees a [hundred] fathoms in length: for lofty in sooth were the woods of gloomy Untola. And all this they heaped for the burning of Kullervo.

They kindled the flame beneath the wood and the great bale-fire crackled and the smell of logs and acrid smoke choked them wondrously and then the whole blazed up in red heat and thereat they thrust Kullervo in the midst and the fire burned for two days and a third day and then sat there the boy knee-deep in ashes and up to his elbows in embers and a silver coal-rake he held in his hand and gathered the hottest fragments around him and himself was unsinged.

Untamo then in blind rage seeing that all his sorcery availed nought had him hanged shamefully on a tree. And there the child of his brother Kalervo dangled high from a great oak for two nights and a third night and then Untamo sent at dawn to see whether Kullervo was dead upon the gallows or no. And his servant returned in fear: and such were his words: 'Lord, Kullervo has in no wise perished as yet: nor is dead upon the gallows, but in his hand he holdeth a great knife and has scored wondrous things therewith upon the tree and all its bark is covered with carvings wherein chiefly is to be seen a great fish (now this was Kalervo's sign of old) and wolves and bears and a huge hound such as might even be one of the great pack of Tuoni.'

Now this magic that had saved Kullervo's life was the last hair of Musti: and the knife was the great knife Sikki: his father's, which his mother had given to him: and thereafter Kullervo treasured the knife Sikki beyond all silver and gold.

Untamoinen felt afraid and yielded perforce to the great magic that guarded the boy, and sent him to become a slave and to labour for him without pay and but scant fostering: indeed often would he have starved but for Wanōna who, though Unti treated her scarcely better, spared her brother much from her little. No compassion for these twins did their elder brother and sister show, but sought rather by subservience to Unti to get easier life for themselves: and a great resentment did Kullervo store up for himself and daily he grew more morose and violent and to no one did he speak gently but to Wanōna and not seldom was he short with her.

So when Kullervo had waxed taller and stronger Untamo sent for him and spake thus: 'In my house I have retained you and meted wages to you as methought thy bearing merited – food for thy belly or a buffet for thy ear: now must thou labour and thrall or servant work will I appoint for you. Go now, make me a clearing in the near thicket of the Blue Forest. Go now.' And Kuli went. But he was not ill pleased, for though but of two years he deemed himself grown to manhood in that now he had an axe set in hand, and he sang as he fared him to the woodlands.

Song of Sākehonto in the woodland:

Now a man in sooth I deem me
Though mine ages have seen few summers
And this springtime in the woodlands
Still is new to me and lovely.
Nobler am I now than erstwhile
And the strength of five within me
And the valour of my father
In the springtime in the woodlands
Swells within me Sākehonto.
O mine axe my dearest brother –
Such an axe as fits a chieftain,
Lo we go to fell the birch-trees
And to hew their white shafts slender:
For I ground thee in the morning
And at even wrought a handle;
And thy blade shall smite the tree-boles
And the wooded mountains waken
And the timber crash to earthward
In the springtime in the woodland
Neath thy stroke mine iron brother.

And thus fared Sākehonto to the forest slashing at all that he saw to the right or to the left, him recking little of the wrack, and a great tree-swathe lay behind him for great was his strength. Then came he to a dense part of the forest high up on one of the slopes of the mountains of gloom, nor was he afraid for he had affinity with wild things and Mauri's [Musti's] magic was about him, and there he chose out the mightiest trees and hewed them, felling the stout at one blow and the weaker at a half. And when seven mighty trees lay before him on a sudden he cast his axe from him that it half cleft through a great oak that groaned thereat: but the axe ~~held~~ there quivering.

But Sāki shouted, 'May Tanto Lord of Hell do such labour and send Lempo for the timbers fashioning.'

And he sang:

> Let no sapling sprout here ever
> Nor the blades of grass stand greening
> While the mighty earth endureth
> Or the golden moon is shining
> And its rays come filtering dimly
> Through the boughs of Saki's forest.
> Now the seed to earth hath fallen
> And the young corn shooteth upward
> And its tender leaf unfoldeth
> Till the stalks do form upon it.
> May it never come to earing
> Nor its yellow head droop ripely
> In this clearing in the forest
> In the woods of Sākehonto.

And within a while came forth Ūlto to gaze about him to learn how the son of Kampo his slave had made a clearing in the forest but he found no clearing but rather a ruthless hacking here and there and a spoilage of the best of trees: and thereon he reflected saying, 'For such labour is the knave unsuited, for he has spoiled the best timber and now I know not whither to send him or to what I may set him.'

But he bethought him and sent the boy to make a fencing betwixt some of his fields and the wild; and to this work then Honto set out but he gathered the mightiest of the trees he had felled and hewed thereto others: firs and lofty pines from blue Puhōsa and used them as fence stakes; and these he bound securely with rowans and wattled: and made the tree-wall continuous without break or gap: nor did he set a gate within it nor leave an opening or chink but said to himself grimly, 'He who may not soar swift aloft like a bird nor burrow like the wild things may never pass across it or pierce through Honto's fence work.'

But this over-stout fence displeased Ūlto and he chid his slave of war for the fence stood without gate or gap beneath, without chink or crevice resting on the wide earth beneath and towering amongst Ukko's clouds above.

For this do men call a lofty Pine ridge 'Sāri's hedge'.

'For such labour,' said Ūlto, 'art thou unsuited: nor know I to what I may set thee, but get thee hence, there is rye for threshing ready.' So Sāri got him to the threshing in wrath and threshed the rye to powder and chaff that the winds of Wenwe took it and blew as a dust in Ūlto's eyes, whereat he was wroth and Sāri fled. And his mother was feared for that and Wanōna wept, but his brother and elder sister chid them for they said that Sāri did nought but make Ūlto angered and of that anger's ill did they all have a share while Sāri skulked the woodlands. Thereat was Sāri's heart bitter, and Ūlto spake of selling as a bond slave into a distant country and being rid of the lad.

His mother spake then pleading, 'O Sārihontō if you fare abroad, if you go as a bond slave into a distant country, if you perish among unknown men, who will have thought for thy mother or daily tend the hapless dame?' And Sāri in evil mood answered singing out in light heart and whistling thereto:

> Let her starve upon a haycock
> Let her stifle in the cowbyre

And thereto his brother and sister joined their voices saying,

> Who shall daily aid thy brother?
> Who shall tend him in the future?

To which he got only this answer,

> Let him perish in the forest
> Or lie fainting in the meadow.

And his sister upbraided him saying he was hard of heart, and he made answer. 'For thee treacherous sister though thou be a daughter of Keime I care not: but I shall grieve to part from Wanōna.'

Then he left them and Ūlto thinking of the lad's size and growing strength relented and resolved to set him yet to other tasks, and is it told how he went to lay his largest drag-net and as he grasped his oar asked aloud, 'Now shall I pull amain with all my vigour or with but common effort?' And the steersman said: 'Now row amain, for thou canst not pull this boat atwain.'

Then Sāri Kampa's son rowed with all his might and sundered the wood rowlocks and shattered the ribs of juniper and the aspen planking of the boat he splintered.

Quoth Ūlto when he saw, 'Nay, thou understandst not rowing, go thresh the fish into the dragnet: maybe to more purpose wilt thou thresh the water with thresh-ing-pole than with foam.' But Sāri as he was raising his pole asked aloud, 'Shall I thresh amain with manly vigour or but leisurely with common effort threshing with the pole?' And the net-man said, 'Nay, thresh amain. Wouldst thou call it labour if thou threshed not with thy might but at thine ease only?' So Sāri threshed with <u>all</u> his might and churned the water to soup and threshed the net to tow and battered the fish to slime. And Ūlto's wrath knew no bounds and he said, 'Utterly useless is the knave: what-soever work I give him he spoils from malice: I will sell him as a bond-slave in the Great Land. There the Smith Āsemo will have him that his strength may wield the hammer.'

And Sāri wept in wrath and in bitterness of heart for his sundering from Wanōna and the black dog Mauri. Then his brother said, 'Not for thee shall I be weeping if I hear thou has perished afar off. I will find himself a brother better than thou and more comely too to see.' For Sāri was not fair in his face but swart and illfavoured and his stature assorted not with his breadth. And Sāri said,

> Not for thee shall I go weeping
> If I hear that thou hast perished:
> I will make me such a brother –

with great ease: on him a head of stone and a mouth of sallow, and his eyes shall be cranberries and his hair of withered stubble: and legs of willow twigs I'll make him and his flesh of rotten trees I'll fashion – and even so he will be more a brother and better than thou art.'

And his elder sister asked whether he was weeping for his folly and he said nay, for he was fain to leave her and she said that for her part she would not grieve at his sending nor even did she hear he had perished in the marshes and vanished from the people, for so she should find herself a brother and one more skilful and more fair to boot. And Sāri said, 'Nor for you shall I go weeping if I hear that thou hast perished. I can make me such a sister out of clay and reeds with a head of stone and eyes of cranberries and ears of water lily and a body of maple, and a better sister than thou art.'

Then his mother spake to him soothingly.

> Oh my sweet one O my dearest
> I the fair one who has borne thee
> I the golden one who nursed thee
> I shall weep for thy destruction
> If I hear that thou hast perished

And hast vanished from the people.
Scarce thou knowest a mother's feelings
Or a mother's heart it seemeth
And if tears be still left in me
For my grieving for thy father
I shall weep for this our parting
I shall weep for thy destruction
And my tears shall fall in summer
And still hotly fall in winter
Till they melt [the] snows around me
And the ground is bared and thawing
And the earth again grows verdant
And my tears run through the greenness.
O my fair one O my nursling
Kullervoinen Kullervoinen
Sārihonto son of Kampa.

But Sāri's heart was black with bitterness and he said, 'Thou wilt weep not and if thou dost, then weep: weep till the house is flooded, weep until the paths are swimming and the byre a marsh, for I reck not and shall be far hence.' And Sāri son of Kampa did Ūlto take abroad with him and through the land of Telea where dwelt Āsemo the smith, nor did Sāri see aught of Oanōra [Wanōna] at his parting and that hurt him: but Mauri followed him afar off and his baying in the nighttime brought some cheer to Sāri and he had still his knife Sikki.

And the smith, for he deemed Sāri a worthless knave and uncouth, gave Ūlto but two outworn kettles and five old rakes and six scythes in payment and with that Ūlto had to return content not.

And now did Sāri drink not only the bitter draught of thralldom but eat the poisoned bread of solitude and loneliness thereto: and he grew more ill favoured and crooked, broad and illknit and knotty and unrestrained and unsoftened, and fared often into the wild wastes with Mauri: and grew to know the fierce wolves and to converse even with Uru the bear: nor did such comrades improve his mind and the temper of his heart, but never did he forget in the deep of his mind his vow of long ago and wrath with Ūlto, but no tender feelings would he let his heart cherish for his folk afar save a[t] whiles for Wanōna.

Now Āsemo had to wife the daughter [of] Koi Queen of the marshlands of the north, whence he carried magic and many other dark things to Puhōsa and even to Sutsi by the broad rivers and the reed-fenced pools. She was fair but to Āsemo alone sweet. Treacherous and hard and little love did she bestow on the uncouth thrall and little did Sāri bid for her love or kindness.

Now as yet Āsemo set not his new thrall to any labour for he had men enough, and for many months did Sāri wander in wildness till at the egging of his wife the smith bade Sāri become his wife's servant and do all her bidding. And then was Koi's daughter glad for she trusted to make use of his strength to lighten her labour about the house and to tease and punish him for his slights and roughness towards her aforetime.

But as may be expected, he proved an ill bondservant

and great dislike for Sāri grew up in his [Āsemo's] wife's heart and no spite she could wreak against him did she ever forego. And it came to a day many and many a summer since Sāri was sold out of Dear Puhōsa and left the blue woods and Wanōna, that seeking to rid the house of his hulking presence the wife of Āsemo pondered deep and bethought her to set him as her herdsman and send him afar to tend her wide flocks in the open lands all about.

Then set she herself to baking: and in malice did she prepare the food for the neatherd to take with him. Grimly working to herself she made a loaf and a great cake. Now the cake she made of oats below with a little wheat above it, but between she inserted a mighty flint – saying the while, 'Break thou the teeth of Sāri O flint: rend thou the tongue of Kampa's son that speaketh always harshness and knows of no respect to those above him. For she thought how Sāri would stuff the whole into his mouth at a bite, for greedy he was in manner of eating, not unlike the wolves his comrades.

Then she spread the cake with butter and upon the crust laid bacon and calling Sāri bid him go tend the flocks that day nor return until the evening, and the cake she gave him as his allowance, bidding him eat not until the herd was driven into the wood. Then sent she Sāri forth, saying after him:

> Let him herd among the bushes
> And the milch kine in the meadow:

These with wide horns to the aspens
These with curved horns to the birches
That they thus may fatten on them
And their flesh be sweet and goodly.
Out upon the open meadows
Out among the forest borders
Wandering in the birchen woodland
And the lofty growing aspens.
Lowing now in silver copses
Roaming in the golden firwoods.

And as her great herds and her herdsman got them
afar, something belike of foreboding seized her and she
prayed to Ilu the God of Heaven who is good and dwells in
Manatomi. And her prayer was in the fashion of a song
and very long, whereof some was thus:

Guard my kine O gracious Ilu
From the perils in the pathway
That they come not into danger
Nor may fall on evil fortune.
If my herdsman is an ill one
Make the willow then a neatherd
Let the alder watch the cattle
And the mountain ash protect them
Let the cherry lead them homeward
In the milktime in the even.
If the willow will not herd them
Nor the mountain ash protect them
And the alder will not watch them

Nor the cherry drive them homeward
Send thou then thy better servants,
Send the daughters of Ilwinti
To guard my kine from danger
And protect my horned cattle
For a many are thy maidens
At thy bidding in Manoine
And skilled to herd the white kine
On the blue meads of Ilwinti
Until Ukko comes to milk them
And gives drink to thirsty Kēme.
Come thou maidens great and ancient
Mighty daughters of the Heaven
Come thou children of Malōlo
At Ilukko's mighty bidding
O [Uorlen?] most wise one
Do thou guard my flock from evil
Where the willows will not ward them
Out across the quaking marshland
Where the surface ever shifteth
And the greedy depths are gulping.
O thou Sampia most lovely
Blow the honey-horn most gaily.
Where the alder will not tend them
Do thou pasture all my cattle
Making flowers upon the hummocks:
With the melody of the mead-horn
Make thou fair this heathland border
And enchant the skirting forest

That my kine have food and fodder,
And have golden hay in plenty
And the heads of silver grasses.
O Palikki's little damsel
And Telenda thy companion
Where the rowan will not tend them
Dig my cattle wells all silver
Down on both sides of their pasture
With your straying feet of magic
Cause the grey springs to spout coolly
And the streams that flow by swiftly
And the speedy running rivers
Twixt the shining banks of grassland
To give drink of honey sweetness
That the herd may suck the water
And the juice may trickle richly
To their swelling teeming udders
And the milk may flow in runlets
And may foam in streams of whiteness.
But Kaltūse thrifty mistress
And arrester of all evil,
Where the wild things will not guard them
Fend the sprite of ill far from them
That no idle hands do milk them
And their milk on earth be wasted
That no drops flow down to Pūlu
And that Tanto drink not of it
But that when at Kame at milk tide
Then their milkstreams may be swollen

And the pails be overflowing
And the good wife's heart be gladdened.
O Terenye maid of Samyan
Little daughter of the forests
Clad in soft and beauteous garments
With thy golden hair so lovely
And thy shoon of scarlet leather,
When the cherry will not lead them
Be their neatherd and their shepherd.
When the sun to rest has sunken
And the bird of Eve is singing
As the twilight draweth closer
Speak thou to my horned creatures
Saying come ye hoofed cattle
Come ye homeward trending homeward.
In the house 'tis glad and pleasant
Where the floor is sweet for resting
On the waste 'tis ill to wander
Looming down the empty shorelands
Of the many lakes of Sutse.
Therefore come ye horned creature
And the women fire will kindle
In the field of honeyed grasses
On the ground o'ergrown with berries.

[*The following lines are offset to indicate a change of tone. Kirby's edition does not so distinguish them, but notes in the Argument at the head of the Runo that it contains 'the usual prayers and charms' (Kirby Vol. 2, p. 78). Magoun gives the lines the heading 'Charms for Getting Cattle Home, Lines 273–314' (Magoun, p. 232).*]

Then Palikki's little damsel
And Telenda her companion
Take a whip of birch to scourge them
And of juniper to drive them
From the hold of Samyan's cattle
And the gloomy slopes of alder
In the milktide of the evening.

[*As above, these lines are offset to indicate a shift in tone and
separate them from those preceding. Kirby's Argument notes a
charm for 'protection from bears in the pastures' (p. 78), while
Magoun supplies the heading 'Admonitory Charms Against Bears,
Lines 315–542 (p. 232).*]

O thou Uru O my darling
My Honeypaw that rules the forest
Let us call a truce together
In the fine days of the summer
In the good Creator's summer
In the days of Ilu's laughter
That thou sleepst upon the meadow
With thine ears thrust into stubble
Or conceal thee in the thickets
That thou mayst not hear cowbells
Nor the talking of the herdsman.
Let the tinkling and the lowing
And the ringing in the heathland
Put no frenzy yet upon thee
Nor thy teeth be seized with longing.
Rather wander in the marshes

And the tangle of the forest.
Let thy growl be lost in wastelands
And thy hunger wait the season
When in Samyan is the honey
All fermenting on the hillslopes
Of the golden land of Kēme
Neath the faring bees a-humming.
Let us make this league eternal
And an endless peace between us
That we live in peace in summer,
In the good Creator's summer.

[*As with the other separations, this indentation is offset to indicate a change in tone, in this case the conclusion or peroration of the lady's prayers. Neither Kirby nor Magoun so distinguishes these lines.*]

All this prayer and all this chanting
O then Ukko silver monarch
Hearken to my sweet entreaty.
Bind in leash the dogs of Kūru
And enchain the forest wild things
And in Ilwe set the Sun-star
And let all the days be golden.

Now Āsemo's wife was a great chanter of prayers – and also a most grasping woman and over heedful of her goods: and that is to be understood [by] the length of her prayer to Ilukko and his maidens for her kine which were very fair and sleek.

But now Sāri had gone some way, and set his food into his wallet as he drove the kine over the water meadows and swamps and out across the heathland to the rich edge of the woodland, and ever as he went he was grieving and murmuring to himself and saying 'Woe to me wretched youth, ill and hard going black fortune: wheresoever I turn my path nothing awaits me but idleness and endless gazing at the tails of oxen ever tramping through the marshes and the dreary level country.' Then coming to a slope in the sun he sat him there and rested and took out his lunch and marvelled at its weight and said, 'Wife of Āsemo thou art not wont to dole me out such a weight of food.'

Then he fell athinking of his life and the luxury of this spiteful mistress, and to long for wheaten bread in slices thick with butter and cakes of finest bakery and for a draught other than water for the quenching of his thirst. Dry crusts, thought he, only does she give me for my chewing and oaten cake at best and with this chaff and straw or the bark of fir not seldom mingled: and cabbage whence her cur has eaten all the fat, and then he bethought him of his wild free early days and of Wanone [*sic*] and his folk, and so slept till a bird prating of evening awoke him and [he] drove the cattle to rest and sat him on a hillock and took from his back his wallet.

And he opened it and turned it about, saying 'many a cake without is handsome but within is ill favoured: and is as this: wheat above and oaten behind', and being in heavy mood and not over eager for his food he took his great knife wherewith to cut the cake and it strove through the scanty crust and ground with such force on the flint that its edge was turned and its point snapped: and to this end came Sikki the heirloom of Kampa. And Sāri fell first into white wrath and then into tears for he treasured that heirloom before silver or gold, and said:

> O my Sikki O my comrade
> O thou iron of Kalervo
> Which that hero wore and wielded
> Nought I had to love in sorrow
> But my knife the picture graver.
> And against a stone 'tis broken
> By the spite of that ill woman.
> O my Sikki O my Sikki
> O thou iron of Kalervo.

And evil thoughts whispered to him and the fierceness of the wild came into his heart and with his fingers he wove a design of wrath and vengeance against the fair wife of Āsemo: and taking a switch of birch and of juniper from a thicket he drove all the kine and cattle into the water marshes and trackless morasses. And he called on the wolves and bears each to take a half as their prey and to save him only a bone from the leg of Urula the most aged cow of the herd. And from this he made a great pipe and blew shrilly and strangely upon it: and this was magic of Sāri's own nor do men say whence he learnt: and he sang thus the wolves to cattle and the bears to oxen, and as the sun was westering redly and bending toward the pine-trees nigh the time of milking, he drove the bears and wolves homeward before him, weary and dusty with his weeping on the ground and enchanting of the wild things.

Now when he drew nigh the farmyard he laid his commands upon the beasts that when the smith's wife came to look about her and stooped down to milk them, they should seize her and crunch her in their teeth.

And so he went along the pathway piping broken and strange music from the cow-bone pipe: thrice he blew on the hill slope and six times at the garden wall. And Āsemo's wife marvelled whence the neatherd had gotten his cow bone for his pipe but heeded not overmuch the matter, for long had she awaited the cows for milking. And she gave thanks to Ilu for the return of her herd: and went out and bade Sāri stay his earsplitting din and then said she to Āsemo's mother,

> Mother 'tis the kine need milking.
> Do thou go and tend the cattle
> For meseems I cannot finish
> Kneading dough as I would have it.

But Sāri mocked her saying that no thrifty housewife would send another and [an] old woman to milk the kine. So Āsemo's wife went swiftly to the sheds and set herself to milk her kine, and gazed upon the herd saying, 'Beauteous is the herd to look on and sleek the horned oxen and well filled are the udders of the kine.'

Then she stooped to the milking and lo a wolf sprang at her and a bear seized her in his grim embrace and they tore her fiercely and crunched her bones, and thus was her jesting and mockery and spite repaid, and the cruel wife brought herself to weeping: and Sāri stood by neither exulting nor relenting and she cried to him, 'Ill dost thou most wicked of neatherds to drive bears and mighty wolves to these peaceful yards.' Then Sāri chid her for her ill and spite toward himself and for the breaking of his cherished heirloom.

Then Āsemo's wife wheedling said, 'Come, thou herdboy, dearest herdboy, come thou apple of this homestead, alter thou thy grim resolve and I beg thee lift this magic from me and release the wolf's jaws and the bear's limbs from me. Better raiment will I give you then an you do so, and handsome ornaments, and wheaten bread and butter and the sweetest draughts of milk for your draining: nor shalt thou labour aught for a year and but lightly in the second.'

Then said Sāri, 'If thou diest so mayest thou perish; there is room enough in Amuntu for thee.'

Then Āsemo's wife in death cursed him using his name and [very?] father's and cried on Ukko the highest of Gods to hear her words.

> Woe thou Sāri Kampa's offspring
> Woe thou crooked fated child Nyelid
> Ill thy fortune dark thy faring
> On the roadway of thy lifetime.
> Thou has trod the ways of thralldom
> And the trackless waste of exile
> But thy end shall be more awful
> And a tale to men forever
> Of a fate of woe [and] horror

Worse than anguish in Amuntu.
Men shall hither come from Loke
In the mirklands far to northward
And shall hither come from Same
In the southways of the summer
And shall fare to us from Kēme
And from the Ocean bath to Westward
But shall shudder when they hear them
Thy fate and end of terror.
To woe thou who as [*illegible*]

[*The verse breaks off here without closing punctuation or any
indication that more is intended.*]

But Sāri went away and there she died – the daughter
of Koi even the fair one whom Āsemo the smith primeval
wooed in far Lohiu for seven years. And her cries reached
her husband at his forge and he turned from the smithy
and went to listen in the lane and then with fear at his
heart hastened and looked about the yard and the distant
sound of piping shrill and strange faring away out over
the marshland under the stars came to his ears and nought
else, but to his eyes came soon that evil sight upon the
ground and his soul was darkened deeper than the night
and starless. But Sāri was far abroad in the wild with pipe
of bone and no man might follow for Mauri's magic was
about him. And his own magic ever waxing went with
him too.

And he wandered onwards aimlessly forward for that
night and a day through thickest woodland till the next

night he found himself in the densest timber grounds of Pūhu and it grew stifling dark and he flung himself on the ground and reflected bitterly.

> Wherefore have I been created?
> Who has made me and has doomed me
> Thus 'neath sun and moon to wander
> 'Neath the open sky forever?
> Others to their homes may journey
> That stand twinkling in the even
> But my home is in the forest.
> In the wind halls must I slumber
> And in bitter rain must bathe me
> And my hearth is midst the heather
> In the wide halls of the wind blast
> In the rain and in the weather.
> Never Jumala most holy
> In these ages of the ages
> Form a child thus crooked fated
> With a friendless doom forever
> To go fatherless 'neath heaven
> And uncared by any mother
> As thou, Jumala, hast made me
> Like a wailing wandering seagull,
> Like a seamew in the weather
> Haunting misty rocks and shoreland
> While the sun shines on the swallow
> And the sparrow has its brightness

And the birds of air are joyous
But that is never never happy.
I Sāri am not happy.
O Ilu, life is joyless.
{I was small and lost my ~~mother~~ father
I was young (weak) and lost my mother.
All my mighty race has perished
All my mighty race}

Then into his heart Ilu sent a thought: and he lifted his head and said 'I will slay Ūlto.' And the thought of his father's wrong and his oath and the tears of his whole lifetime came to him and he said 'Gladly will I slay Ūlto.' And as yet was his heart bitter against his own folk too, save Oanōra only, and he thought him fiercely of the red light leaping from Untamo's dwellings and Untamo lying dead on the stained floor of his own grim halls: but Kullervo knew not his way thence for on every side the forest encompassed him; still he fared onward saying 'wait thou, wait thou Untamoinen destroyer of my race; if I find thee then quickly will thy dwelling leap up in flames and the farmlands lie empty and withered.'

As he fared musing an old dame, even the Blue-robed Lady of the Forest met him asking him 'Whither O Kullervo son of Kalervo goest thou so hastily?'

Then Kullervo told her of his desire to quit the forest and wander to the homeland of Untamo and with fire avenge his father's death and his mother's tears.

Then said she, 'Easy it is for thee to journey though the

track be not known to thee through the forest. Thou must follow the river's path and march for two days and a third day when turning to the Northwest thou wilt find a wooded mountain. Fare not towards it lest ill find thee. March on under the shadow often bending to the left when thou comest to another river and when thou hast followed its banks soon thou wilt strike a fair spot and a great glade and over a great leap a triple waterfall foaming. Then you will know thou art halfway. Even so thou must continue pushing up the river toward its source: and the ground will slope against thee and the wood darken and lie in again till for a day you stumble across bleak waste and then soon wilt thou see the blue of woods of Untamo rising afar off: and mayhap these thou hast not yet quite forgotten.'

Then slipped the Woman of the Forest away among the tree boles and Kullervo following the river – for one not very great was nigh – marched for two days and a third day, then turned to Northwest and espied the wooded mountain. And the sun shone upon it and the trees bloomed and the bees seemed a-humming there and the birds singing, and Kullervo tired of the blue shadows of the wood and thought – my quest will wait, for never can Untamo in the end escape me: I will go drink the sunlight and he turned from the forest path into the sun; and was going up the slopes till he came to a wide clearing and on a fallen log in a patch of light amidst the brambles he saw a maiden with her yellow hair all flowing. And the curse of Louhi's daughter was on him and his eyes saw and saw not: and he forgot the slaying of Untamo and strode to the maiden who heeded him not. A garland of flowers was she plaiting and was singing yet wearily and half-sorrowfully to herself.

'O fair one, pride of Earth,' said Kullervo, 'come with me; wander in the forest with me unless indeed thou be a daughter of Tapio and no human maiden: but even so do I desire thee to be my comrade.'

And the maid was affright and shrank from him. 'Death walketh with thee, wanderer, and woe is at thy side.'

And Kullervo was wroth; but very fair was the maiden and he said "Tis not good for thee to be alone in the forest; nor does it please me; food will I bring thee and fare abroad to lay and lie in wait for thee, and gold and raiment and many things of cost will give thee.'

'Though I be lost in the evil woods, and Tapio has me fast in his hold,' said she, 'yet would I never wish to roam with such as thee, villain. Little does thy look consort with maidens. But thou wouldst, an thou were honest aid me to find the homeward road to my folk which Tapio hides from me.'

But Kullervo was wroth in that she had reviled his un-gainliness, and put kind thought from him and cried: 'Lempo seize thy folk and swift would I put them to the sword didst I come upon them, but thou I wilt have, nor shalt thou dwell in thy father's house again.'

Whereat she was adread and sped like a wild thing of the woods through the tangle from him and he angry after her: till he laid hands upon her and bore her in his arms away in the depths of the woods.

Yet was she fair and he loving with her, and the curse of the wife of Ilmarinen [*sic*] upon them both, so that not long did she resist him and they abode together in the wild till on a day even as Jumala brought the morning, the damsel resting in his arms spake unto him questioning him and said,

> Tell me now of all thy kinfolk
> Of the brave race that thou springst from:–
> Yea, a mighty race it seems me
> Thine is, and a mighty father.

And Kullervo's answer was thus:

[*These lines are offset apparently to indicate a change in speaker.*]

> Nay my race is not a great one
> Not a great one nor a small one:
> I am just of middle station;
> Kalervo's unhappy offspring
> Uncouth boy and ever foolish
> Worthless child and good for nothing.
> Nay but tell me of thy people
> Of the brave race whence thou comest.
> Maybe a mighty race has born thee
> Fairest child of mighty father.

And the girl answered quickly (nor let Kullervo see her face),

> Nay my race is not a great one
> Not a great one nor a small one

I am just of middle station
Wandering maiden ever foolish
Worthless child and good for nothing.

Then stood she up and gazing in woe at Kullervo with outstretched hand and her hair falling about her cried,

To the wood I went for berries
And forsook my tender mother.
Over plains and heath to mountains
Wandered two days and a third one
Till the pathway home I found not.
For the paths led ever deeper
Deeper deeper into darkness
Deeper deeper into sorrow
Into woe and into horror.
O thou sunlight O thou moonbeam
O thou dear unfettered breezes
Never never will I see thee
Never feel thee on my forehead.
For I go in dark and terror
Down to Tuoni to the River.

And before he could leap up and grasp her she sped across the glade (for they abode in a wild dwelling nigh to the glade spoken to him by the Blue Forest Woman) like a shivering ray of light in the dawn light scarce seeming to touch the green dewy grass till she came to the triple fall and cast her over it down its silver column to the ugly depths even as Kullervo came up with her and her last wail he heard and stood heavy bent on the brink as a lump of rock till the sun rose and thereat the grass grew green, birds sang and the flowers opened and midday passed and all things seemed happy: and Kullervo cursed them, for he loved her.

And the light waned and foreboding gnawed at his heart for something in the maiden's last speech and murmur and her bitter ending wakened old knowledge in his heart spell-blind and he felt he would burst for grief and sorrow and heavy fear. Then red anger came to him and he cursed and seized his sword and [went] blindly in the dark heeding neither falls nor bruises up the river as the Dame had directed, panting as the slopes leant against him till at dawn so terrible his haste

> [*The narrative breaks off at this point, and what follows on the rest of the page is a note-outline of the end of the story, written rapidly and with aberrations in syntax attributable to haste. It is here given in full.*]

He goes to Untola and blindly lays waste to everything, gathering an army of bears and wolves together who vanish in the evening and slay the following Musti outside his vill[age]. When everything is destroyed, he flings himself drenched in blood on the bed of Untamo, his self the only house not burnt.

His mother's ghost appears to him and tells him his own brother and sister are amongst those he has slain.

He [is] horror struck but not grieved.

She then tells him that she was [killed] too and he starts

up in a sweat and horror believing he is dreaming and is prostrated when he finds it is not so.

Then she goes on.

(I had a daughter fairest maiden who wandered to look for berries)

Telling how she met a fair distraught maiden wandering with downcast eyes by the bank of Tuoni's river and describes their meeting ending by revealing that it is she who slew herself.

K[ullervo] bites sword hilt in anguish and starts up wildly as his mother vanishes. Then he laments her and goes out setting fire to the hall, passing through the village full of slain into the woods [*in the margin is the note:* 'falls over body of dead Musti'] wailing 'Kivutar' for he has never seen her (as his sister) since he was sold to Ilmarinen. He finds the glade now bleak and desolate and is about to throw himself over same falls when he decides he is not fit to drown in same pools as Kivutar and takes out his sword asking it whether it will slay him.

The sword says if it had joy in the death of Untamo how much in death of even wickeder Kullervo. And it had slaid [*sic*] many an innocent person, even his mother, so it would not boggle over K.

He kills himself and finds the death he sought for.

List of Names

[*The spacing here is as it appears in the manuscript.*]

[*Recto*]

~~Tūva (w. Nyēli)~~   ~~Ulto~~

Kampa (Nyēli)	Ūlto ~~Kem~~
or Kēma	(Puhōsa his land)

Sāaki	Wanōna
or hontō	

Black dog	Mauri
Smith	Āsemo
cf	Āse

Lumya	the Marshland
Teleä	land of Kēme's birth
Kĕmĕnūme	or The Great Land

Ilu Iluko	God of the Sky
	(the good God)

often confused with Ukko   ∴ ran

Amuntu   hell
Tanto   god of hell   Pūh
Lempo   plague & death
also cal[l]ed Qēle or as a [huntsman?]   Kuruwanyo
The great black river of death
                Kūru
Ilwe   Ilwinti   Sky heaven   (Manatomi)
Wanwe   armed goddess
Sutse   the marshland
Samyan   god of the forest
Koi   Queen of [illegible] Lōke

[*Verso*]

the seven daughters of Ilwinti
                Eltelen   Mēlune
    and Saltime
Tekkitai

Malōlo a god   the maker
     of the earth

     Kaltūse
          or

Kampa (*Nyěli*)   Ulko

(Puhōsa   ...)

 Sōki   Wanūna

... Mauri
...   Iemo
    Ase

Lumya   ...land
Telōsa   ...
Kēmi...   ... Great ...
Ilu Iluko   God ...

... Ukko   ...

Amuntu   hell
...   Goddess ... Puli
Lempo   ...
... Qēla   ... Kuruwanyo

Kūru

Iluve Iluvāta... by ... (Manatomi)
...   ...
Sutsu   ... mainland
Samyan   god ...

Kōi green   ...   ... Lōke

3. Draft list of character names
[MS Tolkien B 64/6 folio 6 recto].

VIII 1—16 *

Run 50 —
: 273 — 286
^{312}
*) 43 . kib. complant

Golden Brooch (endowment)!
" trinkle

Finnish Grammar
Kanajestine :

33/254 should it be altered

Reunion : R 31 .143—4 .470 ur idential line
Nairb " 138 GBD — Isvar 584 /515/
530* / 32/275
Old religion ~ myspl. 32/50

mister's important

Cajolery, (5720 In Usar V 215 ft
GBD always only to Isva
Blue (wood)

Reunion
3/54 f.

Comic 33/170
34/9

4. Discontinuous notes and rough plot synopsis
[MS Tolkien B 64/6 folio 21 recto].

Draft Plot Synopses

A loose folio numbered 21 contains discontinuous jotted notes and on both sides rough plot outlines alternative to the continuous narrative. The use of the names Ilmarinen and Louhi is evidence that this precedes the main manuscript.

[*Recto*]

Kalervo and his wife and son and daughter

~~Kullervo a boy child with his father Kalervo~~

The quarrel and raid of Untamo. The homestead laid waste – Kalervo slain ~~and as Kullervo in anguish~~ & all his folk and his wife is carried off by Untamo. She bears Kullervo and a younger sister in sorrow & anguish and tells them of the Tale of Kalervo.

~~Untam~~ Kull. waxed to marvellous strength: his vow as an infant—the knife–(his passionate resentful nature) his ill treatment by Untamo

His only friend his sister.   K's misbehaviour and selling in slavery to Ilmarinen. His utter misery: here he

speaks with wolves in the mountain. carving strange figures
with his father's knife

The cake of Louhi's daughter: Rage and revenge of Kullervo: refuses to loose spell and is cursed by Ilmarinen's
dying wife. He flies from Ilmarinen and goes to destroying
of Untamo: returning from his triumph he meets a maiden
and forces her to dwell with him: he reveals his name and
she runs wailing into the dark and flings herself over the
savage falls.

Kullervo standing in sorrow beside the falls

[*Verso*]

with 36/140—270   Dog Musti
        Quarrelsome mean Kalervo   Kind mother
wretched elder sister & brother.

falls in with the Pohie-Lady of the Forest Who tells him
where his mother is dwelling (give description) with his
brother and daughters.

And he leaves his sorrow and rides to the homestead.
The meeting with his mother: he recounts and she recounts
their ventures[?] lives since her slavery.

He finds his mother wailing, she has sought her younger
and dearly loved daughter for three years in the woods   and
describes her.

Kullervo sees what has happ to his sister

46

and rides recklessly over the ways to the falls where he slays himself.

Or he can meet the maiden in the woodland while fleeing from Ilmarinen and to quench his sorrow* go and devastate Untamo and rescue his mother from bondage discover it is his sister and ride back red with the blood of Untamo and slay himself at the Falls.

put the speech of Unt Kuli R. 36/40 ch met Kuli encounter[?] when his mother beseeches him to be more obedient to Untamo as a boy.

(Mother and Brother are glad he's to go. Sister alone sorry)

Or make it thus after flight from Ilma he finds his people — then destroys Untamo gathering an [sic] magic army of his old friends the wolves and bears: Untamo curses enchants him and he wanders blinded through the forest. Comes to a village and sacks it slaying the ancient headsman and his wife and taking as wife by force his daughter.

> Who asking him his lineage he reveals
> she reveals his origin and how he has slain
> both father and mother and despoiled his sister

Lament of Honto 34/240

---

* *Written in margin* 'alay his suspicion aroused by his sister's death'.

5. Further rough plot synopses [MS Tolkien
B 64/6 folio 21 verso].

Notes and Commentary

5 **The Story of Honto Taltewenlen.** An alternate title or
sub-title written in the upper left corner of the first folio:
Honto is one of Tolkien's several by-names for Kullervo (see
below); *Talte* is his by-name for Kalervo (see below); *wenlen*,
a patronymic suffix equivalent to *poika*, is apparently a Tolkien invention based on the Finnish model. *Taltewenlen*
would thus be 'Son of Talte (Kalervo)'.

(Kalervonpoika). *Poika* is a Finnish patronymic suffix, thus
the full name means 'Kalervo's Son', or 'Son of Kalervo'.

when magic was yet new. This phrase, cancelled in the
manuscript, is here retained in brackets, since magic (also
called sorcery) is practised throughout the story by Untamo,
who is described as 'a fell sorcerer and man of power', by
the dog Musti (himself a possessor of magic abilities), and
by Kullervo, who can shape-change animals. *Kalevala* has
numerous references to magic, probably remnants of primitive shamanism and shamanic practices usually performed
through singing. One of the 'big three' heroes of *Kalevala*,
Väinämöinen, has been interpreted as a shaman. He has the

49

epithet 'eternal singer', and defeats a rival magician in a singing contest by singing him into a bog. In Tolkien's story both Untamo and Kullervo 'weave' magic with their fingers. Kullervo also uses music – singing and playing a magic cow-bone pipe.

Sutse. A name of Tolkien's invention intended to replace earlier 'Suomi' (the Finnish name for Finland) in the text. Other replacement names, all written in the left margin of this opening paragraph, include 'Telea' for earlier Karelja, 'the Great Land/Kemenūme' for earlier Russia, and 'Talte' (*see above*) for earlier Kalervo. Asterisks beside both textual and marginal names coordinate the emendations. With the exception of 'Talte', the replacement names become standard, and are more or less consistently used throughout the remainder of the text. These changes offer the clearest evidence of Tolkien's developing tendency to go from merely following the *Kalevala* nomenclature to using names of his own invention.*

Kemenūme (The Great Land). Replaces Russia in the text. May be based on *Kemi*, a river in northern Finland on which stands the town of the same name. But see footnote to entry for 'Sutse'.

Telea. Replaces earlier Karelja. Karelja is a large area on both sides of the Russo-Finnish border, and is the region where most of the narrative *runos* (songs) compiled by Lönnrot were collected.

---

* A circumstance worth noting is that *Kemenūme* appears in very early notes on Qenya as a name for Russia. See also 'Ilu' below.

Kalervo. Father of Kullervo. His name is probably a variant of Kaleva, a Finnish culture-hero and patronymic ancestor whose name survives in *Kalevala* (with locative suffix *-la*, 'place or habitation' thus Land of Kaleva or Land of Heroes), and in that of his descendant Kalervo. Kalervo is also called by Tolkien *Talte, Taltelouhi, Kampa*, and *Kalervoinen*, the last formed with the Finnish diminutive suffix *inen*. In Finnish, a name can occur in several different forms, depending on the use of diminutives. Cp. Untamoinen below.

Untamo. Brother of Kalervo, uncle of Kullervo. He is possessed of magic powers, and is also a sadist and a would-be murderer. Also called *Untamoinen, Unti, Ūlto, Ulko, Ulkho*.

borne in years past both a son and a daughter and was even now again nigh to childbirth. The elder brother and sister of Kullervo appear in *Kalevala* but only enter the story after Kullervo leaves the smith's household. This ignores the fact that Untamo has already destroyed everyone but Kalervo's wife, who is pregnant and delivers Kullervo in captivity. The compiler of *Kalevala*, Elias Lönnrot, apparently combined two separate stories in order to include Kullervo's incest and death. Tolkien repairs the disjuncture by introducing the older brother and sister at the beginning of the story.

6 **black hound Musti.** Tolkien first called the dog Musti, a conventional Finnish dog name based on *musta*, 'black', translating as something like 'Blackie'. Halfway through the draft, he changed the name to Mauri – possibly formed on

Finnish *Muuri/Muurikki*, 'Black one' or 'Blackie', (used of a cow) – then reverted to Musti. I have retained both, with Mauri where it first appears followed by Musti in square brackets.

7 **cruel and worthless carles.** *Carl*: a churl, a rustic, a peasant. Compare Anglo-Saxon *ceorl.* Tolkien's text mixes Anglo-Saxon archaism with Finnish and pseudo-Finnish names.

foully entreated his folk and lands. The word 'entreat', which conventionally has the meaning of 'supplicate' or 'plead with', seems startlingly inapposite in this context. It is not a mistake, however, but Tolkien's deliberate usage of the word in its archaic meaning, as cited in the *Oxford English Dictionary*, of 'treated' or 'dealt with'. The OED gives an example from 1430: 'So betyn (beaten), so woundyd, Entretyd so fuly [foully].'

gloomy halls of Untola. The locative or habitative suffix *la* identifies this as the home of Unto (Untamo).

Kalervo's babes. In *Kalevala* Kullervo discovers late in the story, after escaping the smith, that he has a sister, but the twinning of the siblings in the present narrative is the invention of Tolkien and not in the original.

Kullervo. Tolkien translates the name as 'wrath', a meaning unattested in *Kalevala*, where it is said to be of disputed origin. It appears to be formed off the patronymic Kalervo. Tolkien described his hero as 'hapless Kullervo', and identified him as 'the germ of my attempt to write legends of my own' (*Letters*, p. 345). Kullervo is the earliest of Tolkien's displaced, heroes, orphans and exiles, a succession that will include Túrin (modelled directly on Kullervo), Beren, and Frodo. Tolkien gives his Kullervo a variety of by-names or epithets: *Kuli* (an obvious short form of Kullervo), *Sake*, *Sākehonto*, *Honto*, *Sāri*, *Sārihontō*. Such multiple naming is typical of *Kalevala*, where for example the hero, Lemmin-kainen, has the nicknames *Ahti* ('King of the Waves'), *Ahti-Saarelainen* ('Island-Ahti' or 'Man of the Island'), *Kaukomieli* ('[Handsome] man with a far-roving mind'), *Kaukolainen* ('Man of Faraway Farm').

Wanōna, or 'weeping'. Compare Túrin Turambar's surviving sister, Nienor/Níniel, whose names mean respectively 'mourning' and 'tear-maiden'. Wanōna is a name of Tolkien's own devising, as in *Kalevala* the sister is not named. One early occurrence in the manuscript calls her Welinōre, but this is immediately cancelled and replaced with Wanōna, and the 'W' is also crossed out and 'U' written in above it (Folio 3). The name occurs once as Wanilie (Folio 4). One instance late in the manuscript changes Wanōna to Wanōra (Folio 7), with the 'W' overwritten with 'O', thus Oanōra. Oanōra (for Wanōna) appears again on the verso of Folio 11 in the sentence 'And as yet was his heart bitter against his own folk too save Oanōra only.' The sister is not cited by name in the succeeding portions of the text.

8 **for ill cradle rocking.** The 'for' in this phrase should be taken to mean 'because of'. The tradition that physical mistreatment of an infant could have psychological reper-cussions is an old one. Compare the saying, 'as the twig is bent so grows the tree'.

one generation from the men of magic. Compare with Tolkien's use of the word *magic* in the opening line, 'when magic was yet new'. Kullervo is in touch with ancient shamanic practices.

not yet more than knee-high. Mythic heroes traditionally grow at an accelerated rate. Compare the Greek Hercules and the Irish Cú Chulainn. Wanōna, described as 'wondrous', also grows at an accelerated rate. In this respect, the twins may owe something to the classical Apollo and Artemis, twin children of Leto by Zeus. In some versions of their story both grew to full adulthood within the day of their birth.

9 **hound of Tuoni.** Hounds in mythology are frequently associated with the underworld, either as guardians or as guides. In *Kalevala* Tuoni is Death (personified) also called Lord of Death. His domain is Tuonela, the underworld, so-called from his name plus the locative/habitative suffix *la*.

10 **Tuoni the marshland.** Perhaps an error for Suomi. See entry for 'Sutse' above.

   {and to Kullervo he gave three hairs ...} This entire sentence, cancelled in the manuscript, is retained in the present text since a magic hair of Musti's later saves Kullervo's life.

11 **a [hundred] fathoms.** The word in brackets is illegible in the manuscript, but 'hundred' is used in Kirby's translation.

12 **the great knife Sikki.** In *Kalevala* the knife is not named. In his article 'From adaptation to invention' John Garth cites Tolkien's Etymologies, a root SIK- with the Qenya

and Sindarin derivatives *sikil, sigil*, meaning 'dagger, knife' (*Tolkien Studies* Vol. XI 2014, p. 40, *The Lost Road*, 385).

13 **Now a man in sooth I deem me.** This is the first of the 'chunks of poetry' interspersed among the prose sections which Tolkien described (*Letters*, p. 7) as his narrative style for *The Story of Kullervo*, and there are rough drafts among the note folios. It is in the so-called '*Kalevala* metre', that Tolkien would have known from the Kirby translation, in which he first read *Kalevala*. This is a rendering into English of the Finnish four-beat eight-syllable line, and is most familiar to English-speakers as the metre of Longfellow's *Hiawatha*. It is less monotonous in Finnish. Alternate versions of the poem appear on folios 22 recto and (upside down) on the verso.

14 **Lempo.** Described in Folio 6 as 'plague and desolation'. The name is confusingly close to the *Kalevala* name for *Lempi*, father of the playboy hero Lemminkäinen. Finnish *lempi* is 'erotic love'. Tolkien has borrowed the name but not the meaning.

16 **daughter of Keime.** Obscure. Possibly a reference to Russia, called Kemenūme in the text; alternatively a possible reference to Teleä/Karelja, glossed in Folio 6 as 'land of Kēme's birth'.

17 **the smith Āsemo.** The name *Āsemo* is apparently Tolkien's invention to replace the *Kalevala* name for this character, *Ilmarinen*, formed on *ilma*, 'sky, air'. *Āsemo* may be formed from Finnish *ase*, 'weapon, tool' (he is, after all, a smith) with the suffix *mo*, used to change a noun into a proper

name. In *Kalevala* the smith Ilmarinen has a far greater role, hammering out the lid of the sky and forging the magical Sampo, actions which qualify him as a kind of creator-god, but might have made him too potent a figure for his minor role in Tolkien's story. Mythic heroes such as Kullervo are often fostered out to smiths; for example the Irish Setanta was fostered to the smith Culann from whom he took the name by which he was thenceforth known, Cú Chulainn, 'Hound of Culann'. The Norse hero Sigurd was mentored by the smith Regin. Puhōsa, the smith's homestead, is hard to locate geographically. It is said at various times to be in the Great Lands identified in the opening paragraphs as Russia, but also in Telea, identified with Karelja.

18 **swart and illfavoured.** It is Tolkien's invention to have his hero's angry and resentful internal emotional state externalized in his dark and ugly outward appearance. In *Kalevala*, Kullervo is described as handsome and yellow-haired. Folio 23 recto contains the marginal note 'Kullervo ugly' and beneath it, also in the margin, 'Mauri black'.

20 **thralldom.** Slavery, serfdom, state of bondage. From Anglo-Saxon *thræl*, from Old Norse *thræll*, 'servant'.

daughter [of] Koi Queen of the marshlands. The smith's wife, in *Kalevala* called *Pohjan neiti*, 'North maid, North miss', is unnamed in Tolkien's story, identified only as the daughter of Koi. In Finnish *koi* is not a proper name but a word meaning 'dawn, daybreak', so this usage is Tolkien's invention. Although Koi does not appear in the story, Tolkien describes her in the name-list as 'Queen of Lōke' (see below). Tolkien clearly means the character to be equivalent to Louhi, a major character in *Kalevala*, where she is a sorceress, the Mistress of Pohjola the Land of the North, and the scheming mother of the North maid. The name *Louhi* is a shortened form of *Loviatar*, minus the feminine suffix *tar*. In *Kalevala*, Loviatar is called Death's daughter, the half-blind daughter of Death's Domain. One of Tolkien's name-lists identifies 'Louhiatar' as 'name of smith's wife' (see entry for 'Kivutar' below).

Puhōsa. Untamo's homestead. Also called Puhu, perhaps as a diminutive.

21 **blue woods/Blue Forest.** Finnish *sininen salo* translates literally as 'blue wilderness', but is often translated 'hazy blue wilderness' or 'blue woodland haze', the result of rising mist in forested areas and especially in low-lying ground. Tolkien associates the colour and the phenomenon with mystery and magic – blue Puhōsa, the blue woods round Untamo's dwelling, the Blue Forest of Kullervo's wanderings.

22 **Ilu the God of Heaven.** Also called Iluku and sometimes confused with Ukko. In Tolkien's list of names in Folio 6 (see below) Ilu is identified as the God of the Sky. Contrast with Malōlō below. It is worth noting that *Ilu* is also the initial element in *Ilúvatar*, the Elvish name for the godhead of Tolkien's mythology, the 'Silmarillion'.

Manatomi. Sky, heaven, also called Ilwe, Ilwinti.

Guard my kine. The longest of Tolkien's 'chunks of poetry', this charm to protect cattle follows closely the incantation of equivalent length by the smith's wife in Runo 32 of the

'Kullervo' portion of *Kalevala*, which Tolkien calls the 'splendid kine-song' (see essay and Notes). He clearly felt it to be an important element in both *Kalevala* and his own story. Both passages are testament to the importance of animal husbandry in a subsistence economy, and both, by their naming of the many woodland and nature spirits (though here Tolkien allows himself some poetic invention), give a good picture of the pagan Finnish worldview.

23 **daughters of Ilwinti.** Apparently air spirits, perhaps breezes. *Ilwinti* is formed from *ilma*, 'sky, air.' The mother goddess in *Kalevala* is called *Ilmatar*, 'Maid of the Air' (Magoun), or 'Daughter of the Air' (Kirby); literally 'air maiden' from *ilma* ('air') plus *tar*, the feminine suffix.

Manoine. From its context with 'daughters of Ilwinti,' 'blue meads of Ilwinti,' and 'white kine' (clouds), Manoine is likely to be equivalent to Manatomi as sky or heaven (see Manatomi above).

Ukko. The ancient Finnish thunder-god. The name means 'old man', and the diminutive, *ukkonen*, is a term for thunder. See 'Ilu' above.

children of Malōlō. Folio 6 identifies Malōlō as 'a god, the maker of the earth'. In the preceding lines the daughters are called 'maidens great and ancient', and 'mighty daughters of the Heaven'. They appear to be ancient feminine divinities or spirits.

24 **Palikki's little damsel, Telenda, Kaltūse, Pūlu.** Names apparently of Tolkien's invention.

Kame. Perhaps a variant of Kēme.

25 **Terenye maid of Samyan.** Folio 6 lists Samyan as 'god of the forest', making him the equivalent of (or replacement for) Tapio, whose daughter is Tellervo, also called 'wind spirit'. Terenye could then be either a forest spirit, a dryad, or akin to the daughters of Ilwinti.

And the women fire will kindle. On Finnish farms smudge fires were lit in the evenings, creating smoke to keep away mosquitoes which bothered the cattle.

26 **Honeypaw.** Certain wild animals in Northern Europe, such as the bear and the wolf, were considered so powerful that to speak their names was to invite their appearance, with predictable danger to human life. Thus circumlocutions, by-names or descriptions were often used, such as 'honey-paw', or 'bruin' (brown) or 'winter sleeper', or 'woodland apple' for the bear. All of these appellations are applied to bears in *Kalevala*, where the actual word for 'bear' is *karhu*. Tolkien would use this name himself in a 1929 'letter from Father Christmas', in which the North Polar Bear reveals his 'real name' as 'Karhu'. In Tolkien's poem the smith's wife calls the bear 'Uru' (bear) but she also flatters him with an affectionate-sounding nickname.

27 **Kūru.** In Folio 6 called 'The great black river of death' with possible variant Kuruwanyo. Finnish *kuolema* is 'death', and Tolkien may have formed the name from that base.

30 **neatherd.** An old word for cattleherder. The word *neat* is archaic and obsolete, but is specific in distinguishing cattle

(cows) and oxen from other domestic hoofed animals such as sheep or goats.

31 **Amuntu.** In Folio 6 identified as Hell.

Nyelid. The list of names on Folio 6 gives Nyēli as a by-name for Kampa, which is itself a by-name for Kalervo. *Nyelid* could mean something like 'of the clan of'. But see 'The Etymologies' in *The Lost Road*, where NYEL- is glossed as 'ring, sing, give out a sweet sound. Q *nyello* singer; *nyelle* bell; T *Fallinel* (*Fallinelli*) = Teleri [PHAL]. N *nell* bell; *nella-* sound bells; *nelladel* ringing of bells. Q *Solonyeldi* = Teleri (see SOL); in Telerin form *Soloneldi*'.

32 **Men shall hither come from Loke.** A place-name apparently equivalent to Lohiu. The similarity to Loki, the name of the Old Norse trickster god, may be intentional. An etymological relationship between Loki and Louhi has been suggested, but cannot be demonstrated.

But shall shudder when they hear them. This and the following two lines are syntactically awkward, and seem to require emendation. The fact that they are also metrically irregular begs for poetic as well as grammatical smoothing. The word I have transcribed as 'hear' (and it certainly looks like it) yet has the 'h' ascender firmly crossed like a 't'. Logically, 'hear them' should be followed by 'of': 'hear them of thy fate', but 'of' is not there. 'To' is jotted in the margin to the left of, and (confusingly) between, the last two lines. It is capitalized, as if beginning a sentence, but it works better after 'Woe', and the final word (or words) is/are illegible. A workable emendation would be 'But shall shudder when they hear them/ [of] thy fate and end [it is written 'and'] of terror./ Woe to thou who . . .'

far Lohiu. Etymologically similar to 'Louhi' and 'Louhiatar' but here clearly referring to a place, not a personage. See entry for 'Lōke' below.

33 **Jumala most holy.** In *Kalevala* Jumala is a sacred being, often translated as 'God', 'God on high', or 'Creator'. Perhaps originally a pagan figure but assimilated to Christianity.

34 **I was small and lost my ~~mother~~ father / I was young (weak) and lost my mother.** Cancelled in the manuscript, the lines are a near direct quote from Kirby's translation of *Kalevala*: 'I was small, and lost my father, I was weak, and lost my mother.' They are retained here as a possible indication of Tolkien's personal interest in what he called 'a very great story and most tragic'. The parallel with Tolkien's own life – his father died when he four years old, his mother when he was twelve – is self-evident.

Blue-robed Lady of the Forest/Woman of the Forest/Blue Forest Woman. The first title follows that of Kirby's translation, and Tolkien has added variations on the epithet. Magoun's translation has 'green-robed maid of the thicket', Friburg's has 'blue-robed matron of the forest'. The mistress of the forest, traditionally named as *Mielikki*, is the consort or wife of Tapio, a major woodland deity. The world of *Kalevala* is full of nature spirits, woodland demi-gods who appear when needed. This one has a particularly portentous role, since it is when Kullervo disobeys her instructions to avoid the mountain that he has the fated meeting with his sister.

35 **Louhi's daughter.** Almost certainly an error for 'Koi's daughter', the smith's wife.

36 **daughter of Tapio.** A dryad, a woodland spirit.

Tapio. God of the forest.

37 **the wife of Ilmarinen.** A mistake for Āsemo. Ilmarinen is the smith in *Kalevala* and Tolkien originally kept the name, then changed it to Āsemo (see above).

40 **wailing 'Kivutar'** Kullervo's sister apparently was at one stage of composition to have had the name (possibly a nickname) *Kivutar*. At the top of Folio 22 verso is written a brief list of names:

Kalervo	>	Paiväta	
Kiputyltö		maiden of pain	his wife;
Kivutar		daughter of pain	his daughter.
Louhiatar		name of Smith's wife	
Saari		Kalervoinen	the hero

Both Kiputyltö and Kivutar are formed from Finnish *kipu*, 'pain'. In his translation of *Kalevala* Friburg calls Kiputyltö 'Pain Maiden'; Magoun calls her 'Pain Girl' and translates *Kivutar* as 'Pain Spirit' and identical with 'Pain Girl' (i.e. 'maiden of pain.'). Kirby leaves the names untranslated.

Introduction to the Essays

Unlike the story, Tolkien's essay on the *Kalevala* exists in two states, one a rough draft manuscript with paragraphs numbered for reorganization, and the other a fair copy typescript. They are catalogued together as Bodleian Library MS Tolkien B 61, folios 126–60. The manuscript, in ink over pencil and heavily emended, consists of twenty-four not always consecutive pages plus an additional, smaller folio (not included here) containing fragmentary jotted notes on both sides. The typescript, which has only occasional emendations in ink, is on lined paper with ruled margins. The text comprises nineteen single-spaced pages, and breaks off in mid-sentence at the very bottom of page 19.

The hand-written title page to the manuscript (Plate 6) reads 'On "The Kalevala" or Land of Heroes', and also bears the notations '(C.C. Coll. [Corpus Christi College] Oxford 'Sundial' Nov. 1914)' and 'Exeter Coll. Essay Club. Feb. 1915', the two dates on which Tolkien is known to have delivered the talk. The November 1914 presentation, given a bare month after his October letter to Edith, and the February one given a scant three months later, clearly belong to the same period as the story.

No firm date can be assigned for the somewhat revised typescript draft, which has no separate title page, but only the heading 'The Kalevala'. A reference in the text to the 'late war' would place it after the World War I Armistice of 11 November 1918, and an allusion to the 'League' (presumably the League of Nations formed in 1919–20) would suggest 1919 as a *terminus a quo*. On the basis of comparison with material in Tolkien's early poetry manuscripts and typescripts Douglas A. Anderson suggests 1919–21 (personal communication), while Christina Scull and Wayne Hammond propose a somewhat later, admittedly conjectural dating of '?1921–?1924' (*Chronology*, p. 115). Anderson's date would place the revision at a time when Tolkien was still living in Oxford (he was on the staff of the *New English Dictionary* from November 1918 to the spring of 1920), while the Scull-Hammond three-year time frame would push it to the period when Tolkien was Reader in English Language at Leeds University. In either case, there is no available evidence that this revised version of the talk was ever given.

As with *The Story of Kullervo*, I have edited both essays' transcriptions for smooth reading. Square brackets enclose words or parts of words missing from the text but supplied where necessary for clarity. False starts, cancelled words and lines have been omitted. Also as with the story, I have chosen not to interrupt the texts (and distract the reader) with note numbers, but a Notes and Commentary section follows each essay proper, explaining terms and usages, and citing references.

On
" The Kalevala ",

or
Land of Heroes

(C.C.C. Oxford "Sundial"   Nov. 1914)
Exeter Coll. Essay Club.   Feb. 1915

6. Manuscript title page of the essay,
'On "The Kalevala"', written in J.R.R. Tolkien's
hand [MS Tolkien B 61 folio 126 recto].

On 'The Kalevala'
or
Land of Heroes

[*Manuscript draft*]

I am afraid this paper was not originally written for this society, which I hope it will pardon since I produce it mainly to form a stop-gap tonight, to entertain you as far as possible in spite of the sudden collapse of the intended reader.

I hope the society will also forgive besides its second-hand character its quality: which is hardly that of a paper – rather a disconnected soliloquy accompanied by a leisurely patting on the back of a pet volume. If I continually drop into talking as if no one in the room had read these poems before, it is because no one had, when I first read it; and you must also attribute it to the pet attitude. I am very fond of these poems: they are litterature [*sic*] so very unlike any of the things that are familiar to general readers, or even to those versed in the more curious by paths: they are so un-European and yet could only come from Europe.

Any one who has read this collection of ballads (more

especially in the original which is vastly different to any translation) will I think agree to that. Most people are familiar from the age of their earliest books onward with the general mould and type of mythological stories, legends, Romances that come to us from many sources: from Hellas by many channels, from the Celtic peoples Irish and British, and from the Teutonic (I put these in order of increasing appeal to myself); and which achieve forums, with their crowning glory in Stead's *Books for the Bairns*: that mine of ancient lore. They have a certain style or savour; a something akin to one another in spite of their vast cleavages that make you feel that whatever the difference of ultimate race of those speakers there is something kindred in the imagination of the speakers of Indo-European languages.

Trickles come in from a vague and alien East of course (it is even reflected in the above beloved pink covers) but alien influence, if felt, is more on the final litterary shapes than on the fundamental stories. Then perhaps you discover the Kalevala, (or to translate it roughly: it is so much easier to say) the Land of Heroes; and you are at once in a new world; and can revel in an amazing new excitement. You feel like Columbus on a new Continent or Thorfinn in Vinland the good. When you first step onto the new land you can if you like immediately begin comparing it with the one you have come from. Mountains, rivers, grass, and so on are probably common features to both. Some plants and animals may seem familiar especially the wild and ferocious human species; but it is more likely to be the often almost indefinable sense of newness and strangeness that will either perturb you or delight you. Trees will group differently on the horizon, the birds will make unfamiliar music; the inhabitants will talk a wild and at first unintelligible lingo. At the worst I hope, however, that after this the country and its manners have become more familiar, and you have got on speaking terms with the natives, you will find it rather jolly to live with this strange people and these new gods awhile, with this race of unhypocritical scandalous heroes and sadly unsentimental lovers: and at the last you may feel you do not want to go back home for a long while if at all.

This is how it was for me when I first read the Kalevala – that is, crossed the gulf between the Indo-European-speaking peoples of Europe into this smaller realm of those who cling in queer corners to the forgotten tongues and memories of an elder day. The newness worried me, sticking in awkward lumps through the clumsiness of a translation which had not at all overcome its peculiar difficulties; it irritated and yet attracted: and each time you read it the more you felt at home and enjoyed yourself. When H. Mods should have been occupying all my forces I once made a wild assault on the stronghold of the original language and was repulsed at first with heavy losses: but it is easy almost to see the reason why the translations are not at all good; it is that we are dealing with a language separated by a quite immeasurable gulf in method and expression from English.

There is however a possible third case which I have not

considered: you may be merely antagonistic and desire to catch the next boat back to your familiar country. In that case before you go, which had best be soon, I think it only fair to say that if you feel that heroes of the Kalevala do behave with a singular lack of conventional dignity and with a readiness for tears and dirty dealing, they are no more undignified and not nearly so difficult to get on with as a medieval lover who takes to his bed to weep for the cruelty of his lady, in that she will not have pity on him and condemns him to a melting death; but who is struck with the novelty of the idea when his kindly adviser points out that the poor lady is as yet uninformed in any way of his attachment. The lovers of the Kalevala are forward and take a deal of rebuffing. There is no Troilus to need a Pandarus to do his shy wooing for him: rather here it is the mothers-in-law who do some sound bargaining behind the scenes and give cynical advice to their daughters calculated to shatter the most stout illusions.

One repeatedly hears the 'Land of Heroes' described as the 'national Finnish Epic': as if a nation, besides if possible a national bank theatre and government, ought also automatically to possess a national epic. Finland does not. The K[alevala] is certainly not one. It is a mass of conceivably epic material: but, and I think this is the main point, it would lose nearly all that which is its greatest delight if it were ever to be epically handled. The main stories, the bare events, alone could remain; all that underworld, all that rich profusion and luxuriance which clothe them would be stripped away. The 'L[and] of H[eroes]' is in fact a collection of that delightful absorbing material which, on the appearance of an epic artist, because of its comparative lowness of emotional pitch, has elsewhere inevitably been cast aside and afterwards overshadowed (far too often) has vanished into disuse and utter oblivion.

It is any case to all that body of myth of queer troglodyte story, of wild jugglings with the sun and moon and the origins of the earth and the shapes of Man that in Homer (for instance) has properly been pruned away: it is to this that the Kalevala may be compared, not to the larger grandeur of the epic theme. Or again it is to the quaint tales, the outrageous ghosts, the sorceries and by-tracks of human imagination and belief that crop out here and there in the usually intensely clear air of the sagas that the 'L of H' can be likened, not to the haughty dignity and courage, the nobility of which the greater sagas tell.

But the queer and strange, the unrestrained, the grotesque is not only interesting: it is valuable. It is not always necessary to purge it out altogether in order to attain to the Sublime. You can have your gargoyles on your noble cathedral, but Europe has lost much through too often trying to build Greek Temples.

We have here then a collection of mythological ballads full of that very primitive undergrowth that the litterature of Europe has on the whole been cutting away and reducing for centuries with different and earlier completeness in different peoples. Such a collection would no doubt be the despoil of anthropologists who might luxuriate here awhile. Commentators I know make many notes to their translations, saying 'Compare this story with the one told in the Andaman Isles' or 'Compare that belief with the one shown in the Hausa Folktales' and so forth: but let us avoid this. It after all only proves that Finns and Andaman Islanders are nearly related animals (which we knew before). Therefore let us rather rejoice that we have come suddenly upon a storehouse of those popular imaginings which we had feared lost, stocked with stories as yet not sophisticated into a sense of proportion; with no thought of the decent limits even of exaggeration, with no sense, or rather not our sense, of the incongruous (except where we suspect incongruity is delighted in). We are taking a holiday from the whole course of progress of the last three Millenniums: and going to be wildly unhellenic and barbarous for a time, like the boy who hoped the future life would provide for half holidays in Hell, away from Eton collars and hymns.

The glorious exaggerations of these ballads, by way of illustration, recall the method of story telling in the Mabinogion, but really their cases are rather different. In the K[alevala] there is no attempt at plausibility, no cunning concealment of the impossible; merely the child's delight in saying how he has cut down a million trees and slaughtered twenty policemen: which has no thought to take you in but is a primitive hero-story. Of course in the Mab[inogion] there is the same delight in a good story, in a strong swap of imagination but the picture has more technique: its colours are marvellously schemed, its figures grouped. It is not so with L. of H. If a man kills a gigantic elk in one line it may be a she-bear in the next. To elaborate this is unnecessary: but it might be made the occasion of an attempt to say just what I find the atmosphere of the Kalevala to be: which you can correct from your own knowledge, or from the extracts which I would wish to read until your patience was exhausted and you felt the appropriateness of the last remarks of the Kalevala.

'Een the waterfall when flowing /yields no endless stream of water./ Nor does an accomplished singer /sing till all his knowledge fail him.'

What I feel is – that there is no background of litt[erary] tradition. The M[abinogion] has such a background: a feeling of a great amount of devel[opment] which has resulted in a field of the most excellently harmonised and subtly varied colours against which the figures of the actors of the stories stand out; but they also harmonize with the marvellous surrounding colour-scheme and lose in startlingness if not in clearness. Most similar national legend litt[erature] has something of it. The Kalevala to me feels to have none. The colours, the deeds, the marvels, and the figures of the heroes are all splashed onto a clean bare canvas by a sudden hand: even the legends concerning the origins of the most ancient things seem to come fresh from the singer's hot imagination of the moment. There are no ultra modernities like trams or guns or aeroplanes in it: the heroes' weapons it is true are the so-called 'antique' bow and spear or sword but at the same time there is a 'nowness', a quite unhazy unromantic momentariness and presentness that quite startles you, especially when you discover that you are reading all the time of the earth being made out of a teal's egg or the sun and moon being shut up in a mountain.

II

As to what is known of the origin of the Kalevala: ever since the coming of Väinämöinen and his making of the great harp, his Kantele fashioned of pike-bone, from what we know of the Finns they have always been fond of ballads; and those ballads have been handed on and sung day after day with unending zest from father to son and son to grandson down to the present day when, as the ballads now bewail: 'The songs are songs of bygone ages/ hidden words of ancient wisdom/, songs which all the children sing not/ all beyond men's comprehension/ in these ages of unfortune/ when the race is near its ending.' The Shadow of Sweden and then of Russia has been over the country for many centuries. Petrograd is in Finland. But the remarkable and delightful thing is that these 'songs of bygone ages' have not been tinkered with.

Sweden finally in [the] 12th cent[ury] conq[uered] Finland (after contin. warfare combined with some intercourse that stretches back beyond the beg[inning] of our era in which too our own ancestors in Holstein had a good part). Christianity then began slowly to be introduced – in other words the Finns were one of the last acknowledged pagan peoples in Med[ieval] Eur[ope]. The Ka[levala] today is pract[ically] untouched: and except at the end and in a few references to Ukko God of Heaven even hints at the existence of Christianity are almost entirely absent. These largely account for its interest and 'undergrowth' character, though also for its minor emot[ional] key: its narrow and parochial view (things in themselves not without delight).

For another seven cen[turies] the ballads were handed on in spite of Sweden, in spite of Russia and were not written down until Elias Lönnrot in 1835 made a selection of them. These were all collected in Eastern Finland and are consequently in a dialect diff[erent] to that of modern litterary Finnish. This dial[ect] has become a kind of poetic convention. Lönnrot was not the only collector, but it was to him that it occurred to string a selection into loosely connected form – as it would seem from the result with no small skill. He called it the Land of Heroes, Kalevala from Kaleva the mythological ancestor of all the heroes. It consisted of twenty-five Runos (or Cantos): this was enlarged with new collected material to double, and published again in 1849, and almost immediately appeared in translation in other lang[uages].

It is interesting to realize however that this ballad-singing, nevertheless, still goes on: that those ballads here by chance crystallized for us are capable of and still undergo a thousand variations. The Kalevala, too, is by no means all the ballad litt[erature] of Finland and is not even the whole of the collected ballads even of Lönnrot, who published as well a whole volume of them under the name 'Kanteletar' or the 'Daughter of the Harp'. The Kalevala is only different in this that it is connected and so more readable, and covers most of the field of Finnish mythology from the Genesis of Earth and Sky to the depart[ure] of Väinämöinen. The lateness of its collection is apt to make those with a prob[ably] unwholesome modern thirst for the 'authentically primitive' feel doubtful. It is however very likely the real reason why the treasure house remained unrifled: it was not redecorated or upholstered, whitewashed or otherwise spoilt: it was left to the care of chance; to the genius of the fire-side and escaped the pedant and the instructive person.

[Jumala, whose name translates God in the Bible, is still in the Kalevala the God of clouds and rain, the old man of the sky, the guardian of the many Daughters of Creation] – It is very parallel to the interest of Icelandic Bishops in the adventures [of] Thórr and Óðinn; it is hardly an instance as I have heard claimed, of the still-struggling presence of paganism in Modern Eur[ope] under layers of Christianity or later of Hebraic biblicality. Even when collected and at last suffering the fate of reproduction in print these poems by luck escaped being handled roughly or moralistically: it is a startling litterature to be so popular among that now most law-abiding and most Lutheran of Europe's peoples.

III

The language of these poems, Finnish, makes a strong bid for the place of most difficult in Europe: though it is anything but ugly, in fact it suffers like many lang[uages] of

its type from an excess of euphony: so much so that the
music of language is apt to be expended automatically and
leave no excess with which to heighten the emotion of a
lyric passage. Where vowel harmony and the softening
of cons[onants] is an integral part of <u>ordinary speech</u>, there
is less chance for sudden unexpected sweetnesses. It is a
language practically isolated in Europe except for the
related and neighbouring Estonia whose stories and whose
tongue are very closely akin. (I am told it bears relation to
tribal speeches in Russia, to Magyar, to Turkish in the far
distance.) It bears no relation to either of its neighbours
except in process of borrowing: it is too a language of a
type altogether more primitive than most in Europe. It
still partakes of a flexible fluid unfixed state inconceivable
in English. In the poetry meaningless syllables and even
meaningless words that just <u>sound</u> jolly are freely inserted.
In such lines as

> 'Enkä lähe Inkerelle
> Penkerelle Pänkerelle'

or

> 'Ihveniä ahvenia
> Tuimenia Taimenia'

are possible where pänkerelle merely echoes Penkerelle,
and Ihveniä and Tuimenia are merely invented to set off
ahvenia and taimenia.

<u>Its metre</u> is roughly the same as that of the translation
though much freer: octosyllabic lines with about four
stresses (two main ones usually two subordinate). It is of

course the unrhymed trochaic metre of 'Hiawatha'. This was pirated as was the idea of the poem and much of the incident (though none of its spirit at all) by Longfellow – a fact which I merely mention because it is usually kept dark in biographical notices of that poet. 'Hiawatha' is not a genuine storehouse of Indian folklore, but a mild and gentle bowdlerising of the Kalevala coloured I imagine with disconnected bits of Indian lore and perhaps a few genuine names. L[ongfellow]'s names are often too good to be inventions. It was either L[ongfellow]'s second or third journey to Europe (the one whose object was the acquiring of Dan[ish] and Swed[ish]) that connected with the Kal[evala]'s first rush into translations in Scandinavian and German. The pathos, I think, only of the Kalevala finds anything like an equal reflection in its imitator (a gentle mild and rather dull American don the author of Evangeline) 'who the London Daily News (I am now quoting an American appreciation) admitted had produced one of the most marvellous lines in all English: 'Chanting the Hundredth Psalm that Grand old Puritan Anthem.''

This metre, monotonous and thin as it can be, is indeed if well handled capable of the most poignant pathos (if not of more majestic things): I do not mean the 'Death of Minnehaha' but in the Kalevala the 'Fate of Aino' and the 'Death of Kullervo', where it is enhanced, not hindered, by the to us humorous naïveté of the unsophisticated mythological surroundings. Pathos is common in the Kalevala – often very true and keen. One of the favourite subjects – not a majestic one but very well handled – is the other side

to a wedding which the 'happy ever after' style of litt[era-
ture] usually avoids: – the lament and heartsinking even of
a willing bride on leaving her father's house and the familiar
things of home. This in the state of society reflected in the
'Land of Heroes' was evidently near to tragedy, where
mothers-in-law were worse than anywhere in litterature,
and where families dwelt in ancestral homes for generations
– sons and their wives all under the iron hand of the
Matriarch.

If you are bored of the sing-song character of this metre,
as you may well be, it is only well to remember that these
are only accidentally as it were written things; they are in
essence sing-songs chanted to the harp as the singers swayed
backwards and forwards in time. There are many allusions
to this custom: as for instance at the beginning:

> 'Let us clasp our hands together
> Let us interlock our fingers
> Let us sing a cheerful measure
> Let us use our best endeavours
>
> *   *   *   *
>
> And recall our songs and legends
> of the belt of Väinämöinen
> of the forge of Ilmarinen
> and of Kaukomieli's sword point.'

IV

The Religion of these poems is a luxuriant animism – it can hardly be separated from the purely mythological: this means that in the Kalevala every stock and stone, every tree, the birds, waves, hills, air, the tables, swords and the beer even have well defined personalities which it is one of the quaint merits of the poems to bring out with singular skill and aptness in numerous 'speeches in part': The most remarkable of these is the speech of the sword to Kullervo before he throws himself upon its point. If a sword had a character you feel it would be just such as is pictured there: a cruel and cynical ruffian; see Runo 36/330. There is also the mention of a few other cases, the lament of the Birch Tree; or the passage (reminiscent of 'Hiawatha' but better) where Väinämöinen seeks a tree to give him timber for his boat (Runo XVI); or where Lemminkainen's mother seeking for her lost son (R XV) asks all things that she meets for news, the moon, the trees, even the pathway and they answer in characterized parts. This is one of the most essential features of the whole poem: even ale talks on occasion – as in a passage I hope to have time to read, the story of the Origin of Beer (Runo XX 522/546).

The Kalevaläic idea of Beer is often enthusiastically expressed but the oft-repeated 'The Ale is of the finest, best of Drinks for prudent people' implies (as also the rest of the poems do) a certain moderation. The joys of Teutonic drunkenness do not seem to have appealed so much as other vices; though drink's value in setting

free the imagination (and the tongue) was often praised
(Runo 21. 260):

> 'O thou Ale thou drink delicious
> Let the drinkers be not moody
> Urge the people on to singing;
> Let them shout with mouth all golden
> Till our lords shall wonder at it,
> And our ladies ponder o'er it.
> For the songs already falter
> And the joyous tongues are silenced
> When the Ale is ill-concocted,
> And bad drink is set before us;
> Then the minstrels fail in singing
> And the best of songs they sing not,
> And our cherished guests are silent,
> And the cuckoos call no longer.'

But beyond this there is a wealth of mythology; every
tree wave and hill again has its nymph and spirit (distinct
from the character app[arentl]y of each individual object).
There is the nymph of blood and the veins: the spirit of
the rudder: there is Moon and his children, the Sun and
his (they are both masculine). There is a dim and awesome
figure (the nearest approach to regal dignity) Tapio God
of the Forest and his spouse Mielikki, with their fairylike
son and daughter 'Tellervo little maiden of the Forest
clad in soft and beauteous garments' and her brother
Nyyrikki with his red cap and blue coat; there is Jumala or
Ukko in the heavens and Tuoni in the earth or rather in

some vague dismal region beside a river of strange things.

Ahti and his wife Vellamo dwell in the waters and there are a thousand new and quaint characters for acquaintance [–] Pakkanen the frost, Lempo the god of evil, Kankahatar the goddess of weaving – but a catalogue does not I am afraid inspire the unintroduced and bores the others. The division between the offspring of nymphs and sprites – you cannot really call them gods it is much too Olympic – and the human characters is hardly clearly drawn at all. Väinämöinen, most human of liars, most versatile and hardy of patriarchs, who is the central figure, is the son of the Wind and of Ilmatar (daughter of the Air). Kullervo most tragic of peasant boys is but two generations from a swan.

I give you just this jumble of gods great and small to give some impression of the delightful atmosphere into which you plunge in the Kalevala – in case some have never plunged. If you are not of this temperament – or think you are not designed for getting on well with these divine personages, I assure you they behave most charmingly, and all obey the great Rule of the Game in the Kalevala which is to tell at least three lies before imparting any accurate information however trivial. It had become I think a kind of formula of polite behaviour, for no one seems to believe you until your fourth statement (which you modestly preface with 'all the truth I now will tell you, though at first I lied a little'[)].

V

So much for religion, if you can call it such, and the imaginary background. The real scenery of the poems, the place of most of its action is <u>Suomi</u> the Marshland: Finnland [*sic*] as we call it or as the Finns often call it the Land of Ten Thousand Lakes. Short of going there I imagine one could scarcely get a better picture of the land than the Kalevala gives (of the land a century ago at any rate, if not of modern progress): it is instinct with love of it: of its bogs and wide marshes in which stand kind of islands formed by rising ground as by hills topped with trees perhaps. The bogs are always before you or beside you and a worsted or outwitted hero is always thrown into one. One sees the lakes and reed-fenced flats with slow rivers: the perpetual fishing: the pile-built houses – and then in winter the land covered with sleighs and men faring over quick and firm alike on snow-shoes.

Juniper, Pine, Fir, aspen, birch, scarce the oak, seldom any other tree, are continually mentioned; and whatever they be nowadays in Finland the bear and wolf are persons of great importance in the 'Kalevala' and many sub-arctic animals besides which we do not know in Britain.

The customs are all strange and the colours: the pleasures and the dangers different: Cold on the whole is regarded with the greatest horror, and perpetual steaming hot baths are one of the greatest daily features. The Sauna or bath-house (a quite separate and elaborate building affixed to all respectable homesteads) has I believe from time immemorial been a charact[eristic] of Finnish dwellings. They take these hot and often.

Society is composed of prosperous households and scattered villages; the poems deal with the highest life but that is only with the life of the richer farmers separated a little from the village. Nothing causes more violent anger to any of the heroes than for his wife to demean herself by going to talk 'down in the village'. It reflects a quiet and moderately contented people but shorn of all the higher and more majestic aspects of national life or tradition: they are governed from above by an alien power. Rarely does such a word as king come in: there is no courtly grandeur, no castles (where they are mentioned it is often mere bad translation).

Patriarchs, stout yeomen with white beards are the most majestic figures to be seen (when their wife is not there). The power of mothers is the most arresting characteristic. Even old Väinämöinen consults his mother on most occasions of difficulty: this tying to the apron-strings goes on even after death; and instructions are issued occasionally from the grave. The housewife's opinion is universally put first. The feelings towards mothers and <u>sisters</u> are far the most genuine and deep and powerful throughout. A confirmed villain of loose morals and wife-beating propensities as the lively Lemminkainen (as he is always called) shows only his best most and affectionate feelings for his mother. The great tragedy of Kullervo (the reckless peasant boy) is one of brother and sister.

Beyond Finland we are often carried in sleighs or

boats, or by more swift and magic means, to Pohja, a mirky misty northland country, sometimes evidently thought of as Lappland, more often it is no one seems clear where, whence magic comes and all manner of marvels; where Luohi [*sic*] dwells who hid the Sun and moon. Sweden, the Lapps, Estonia are often mentioned: Saxony (which is our present enemy) rarely and distantly. Russia our ally not often and usually unpleasantly; of a heartless virago of a wife it is said 'all estranged is now thy brother and his wife is like a Russian'; and of the most desperate and miserable life it is said to be 'as a prisoner lives in Russia only that the jail is wanting'.

VI

I have now tried to suggest without any detailing of plot or retailing of tit-bits to hint at the style and quality of the Kalevala, the Land of Heroes. Its style of course largely depends on all these beliefs and social characteristics I have talked of: there are however some very curious tricks[?] of a more accidental and individual character which so colour the whole that they seem worth mentioning before I cease from my meandering discourse.

There is the curious thing I should like to call 'super-adding' by which after a comparison or even after a statement the next line contains a great enlargement of it, often with reckless alteration of detail or of fact: colours, metals, names are piled up not for their distinct represen-tation of ideas so much as just for the emotional effect.

There is a strange and often effectively lavish use of the words gold and silver, and honey, which are strewn up and down the lines. Colours are rarer; rather do we get gold and silver, moonlight and sunlight, an intense delight in both of which is frequently breaking forth.

There are many such details as these; the incantations, or prayers of deprecation are more essential; they perpetually recur in the presence of any evil or evil feared, and vary from five lines to five hundred, which is the length of the splendid 'Kine-song' of Ilmarinen's wife; while most delightful too are 'songs of origin' – you have only got to know the accurate detailed history of the origin birth and ancestry of anyone (I don't say any <u>thing</u> because there is practically no such distinction for the Kalevala) to have the power to stop the evil and cure the damage he has done or otherwise deal with him. The songs of the 'Origin of Iron' and the 'Origin of Beer' are the most delightful.

To conclude – although it is clear that to our artificial rather over-selfconscious modern taste, a lot of cheap smiles can be got out of these poems (above all out of a bad or mediocre translation) – yet that is not the attitude in which I wish to put them before you. There <u>is</u> a certain humour (in conversation between characters and so forth) which it is justifiable to smile at, but it is really to incur laughter for [our] own weakness, our own dulled vision, as of old age, if we laugh too loftily at the simplicity of the balder passages of the Land of Heroes: unless indeed we laugh for pleasure at the finding of something so fresh and delightful.

But there are passages which are not only entertaining

stories of magic and adventure, quaint myths, or legend; but which are truly lyrical and delightful even in translation, and this high poetical feeling is continually occurring in lines, or couplets, or numbers of lines up and down the Runos but so unlevel as to make purple passage quot[ation] useless. The episodes too and situations are by no means inferior (often vastly superior) to the ballads of much more famous countries than Finland. We are dealing with a popular poetry: overburdened with no technique; unconscious and uneven.

But the delight of Earth, the wonder of it; the essential feeling as of the necessity for magic; that juggling with the golden moon and silver sun (such are they) that is man's universal pastime: these are the things to seek in the Kalevala. All the world to wheel about in, the Great Bear to play with and Orion and the Seven Stars all dangling magically in the branches of a silver birch enchanted by Väinämöinen; the splendid sorcerous scandalous villains of old to tell of when you have bathed in the 'Sauna' after binding the kine at close of day into pastures of little Suomi in the Marshes.

[*The formal text apparently ends here, but the following page is clearly sequential and contains an introduction and notes for passages to be read aloud.*]

VII

<u>Quotation</u>
The translation I am going to use is that of the 'Everyman' series (2 vols) W.H. Kirby: who sometimes seems to plump unnecessarily for the prosy and verbally preposterous, though the great difficulty of course, of the original style is hard to exaggerate. As far as I can see he seems to have tried as nearly as possible the task of making each line correspond to each line of the original which hasn't improved things: but occasionally he is very good indeed.

If anyone does not know the story (and there is time) I can scarcely do better than read the bald summary in the preface to this edition.

Passages:

The favourites among the Finns are the episodes of 'Aino' and 'Kullervo'

1) <u>Aino</u> R. III 530 (*circa*) to end: R. IV (140–190) 190–470

2) <u>Kullervo</u> R. <u>31</u>:. 1–200 <u>34</u> 1–80 <u>35</u> (170) 190–290 <u>36</u> (60–180) 280–end

3) <u>The</u> '<u>Kine-Song</u>' (cp. above page)
<u>32</u> 60–160 210–310

(This includes the classic example of 'wheedling': the bear of course is the most hated of all animals to the farmer's wife: this is how she addresses him. 32 310–370;. 390–430;. 450–470)

4) Origin of Iron <u>IX</u> 20–260

5) Origin of Beer <u>XX</u> 140–250:. 340–390

6) Forging of Sampo X 260–430

7) Great Ox XX 1–80

8) Joukahainen III 270–490

9) Tormenting of the Bride <u>XXII</u> 20–120; (130–190)
   (290–400)

Notes and Commentary

67 **not originally written for this society.** See Introduction to the Essays. Tolkien first delivered this talk to the Sundial Society of Corpus Christi College, Oxford, on 22 November 1914. He gave it again to the Essay Club of Exeter College in February of 1915.

the sudden collapse of the intended reader. I have been unable to find any further information on the identity of the reader or the nature of the collapse.

litterature. Tolkien uses this spelling throughout, chiefly in abbreviations, as 'litt'.

68 **the original which is vastly different to any translation.** While at Exeter College, Tolkien checked out C.N.E. Eliot's *A Finnish Grammar* from the library in order to try to read *Kalevala* in its original language. He was already, it would seem, working on the theory expressed in Manuscript A of 'On Fairy-stories' that 'Mythology is language and language is mythology' (*Tolkien On Fairy-stories*, p. 181).

Stead's *Books for the Bairns*. A series of books for young people published by W.T. Stead, an English journalist, philanthropist and politician. *Books for the Bairns* repackaged classics, fairy tales, fables, nursery rhymes, Great Events in British History, and the Gospels, giving them all a moral and Christian perspective aimed at reforming the world. *Books for the Bairns*, First Series 1806–1920, were well-known to young people of Tolkien's generation.

Indo-European languages. The Indo-European language theory, derived from nineteenth-century comparative philology and mythology, reconstructed by phonological correspondences and principles of sound-change a hypothetical pre-historic language called Proto-Indo-European from which the modern Indo-European language families have descended. Finnish, related to Hungarian and (distantly) to Turkish is not Indo-European but Finno-Ugric.

the above beloved pink covers. While there are no pink covers mentioned 'above', Tolkien's later typewritten essay notes that Stead's *Books for the Bairns* had pink covers.

Thorfinn in Vinland the good. Thorfinn Karlsefni was an eleventh-century Icelander who tried to establish a colony in 'Vinland', previously so named by Leif Eríksson and thought to be somewhere on the north-east coast of North America. His expedition is mentioned in two fourteenth-century Icelandic manuscripts, the *Hauksbók* (Book of Haukr), and the *Flateyjarbók* (Flat-island Book).

69 **when I first read the Kalevala.** According to both Humphrey Carpenter and John Garth, Tolkien first read Kirby's trans-

lation some time in 1911, his last year at King Edward's School. He went up to Oxford in the autumn of that year, and checked out Charles Eliot's *Finnish Grammar* from the Exeter College Library.

the clumsiness of a translation. Not only did Tolkien dislike Kirby's translation, his stated principle that 'Mythology is language and language is mythology' (see entry for 'original translation' above) would invalidate any translation of a work as faithfully representing the original.

H. Mods. Classical Honour Moderations, a first round of examinations at Oxford University, in which the student can get a First (highly desirable), a Second (good but not great), and a Third (a weak pass). Tolkien got a Second.

70 **Troilus to need a Pandarus.** Tolkien could be thinking of the story as told in Chaucer's poem *Troilus and Criseyde* or in Shakespeare's play *Troilus and Cressida*. In both works, Cressida's uncle, Pandarus, acts as go-between for the lovers.

71 **queer troglodyte story.** The primary meaning of troglodyte is 'cave-dweller' (from Greek *trogle*, 'hole', with the extended sense 'hermit'). Tolkien presumably meant a story which has been isolated from the rest of society. Also see the usage by Andrew Lang in the entry below for Andaman Isles.

72 **Andaman Isles.** The Andaman Isles, a territory of India, are situated in the Indian Ocean halfway between the Indian subcontinent and Southeast Asia. In *Custom and Myth*, Andrew Lang twice refers to Andaman Islanders, first querying: 'If a tertiary troglodyte was like a modern Andaman Islander . . . would he stand and meditate in awe on the fact

that a tree was taller than he . . .?' (p. 233); and next suggesting that, 'If the history of religion and of mythology is to be unravelled, we must examine what the unprogressive classes in Europe have in common with Australians and Bushmen and Andaman Islanders' (p. 241). Worth noting is Tolkien's much later suggestion in both the A and B drafts of 'Beowulf: The Monsters and the Critics' (conjecturally dated by Michael Drout to c. 1933–35) that contemporary critics might substitute 'Andaman-islanders . . . for Anglo-Saxons' (*Beowulf and the Critics*, pp. 33, 81).

Hausa Folktales. The Hausa are a Sahelian people occupying a territory ranging over Northeastern Nigeria and Southeastern Niger. In *The British Folklorists: A History*, Richard Dorson notes that 'Within a five-year period, 1908–1913, four folklore and language collections were published on the Hausa' (p. 368). Dorson cites Major Arthur John Newman Tremearne's *Hausa Folktales*, published in 1914. An article entitled 'Hausa Folktales' by 'F.W.H.M.' was published in the journal *African Affairs*, Oxford University Press, 1914; XIII 457. Appearing at the time when Tolkien was writing, these sources would have been available to him. The skeptical view of comparative mythology here expressed foreshadows Tolkien's later and equally dismissive opinion of the comparative approach in his essay 'On Fairy-stories'.

the Mabinogion. The great literary repository of Welsh mythology. It exists for the most part in two manuscripts, the White Book of Rhydderch (*Llyfr Gwyn Rhydderch*, AD 1300–1325) and the Red Book of Hergest (*Llyfr Coch*

Hergest, 1375–1425). It was translated into English by Lady Charlotte Guest in 1838–49. Tolkien had copies of all three volumes in his library.

74 **Väinämöinen.** The primeval singer and oldest culture-hero, first of the 'big three' heroes of *Kalevala*, the other two being Ilmarinen the smith and Lemminkainen the rascally playboy. Väinämöinen is the first-born and most folkloric of the three, having aspects of shamanism in his character.

Petrograd is in Finland. Tolkien is speaking geographically, not politically, though in the case of Finland the two often overlap, since Finland became a Grand Duchy of Russia in 1809. Petrograd (changed from St. Petersburg in 1914) is at the head of the Gulf of Finland, at the base of the Karelian isthmus. Karelia, which has a large Finnish population, is divided now between Finland and Russia. Many of the runos collected by Lönnrot, especially those concerning Kullervo, came from Karelia.

75 **Elias Lönnrot in 1835 made a selection.** In 1835 Elias Lönnrot, a Finnish physician and folklore collector, published a selection from his extensive collection of *runos* or songs, now called the *Old Kalevala*.

Lönnrot was not the only collector. Earlier collectors included Zachris Topelius, Matthias Castrén, Julius Krohn, and Krohn's son Kaarle Krohn. For a complete discussion see Domenico Comparetti, *Traditional Poetry of the Finns*, London: Longmans Green, 1898, and Juha Pentikäinen, *Kalevala Mythology*, trans. Ritva Poom, Indiana University Press, 1989.

published again in 1849. The augmented, standard edition of *Kalevala* from which all current translations are made.

78 'Hiawatha' is not a genuine storehouse of Indian folklore, but a mild and gentle bowdlerising of the Kalevala. For more on this, and for its relation to Tolkien's invented languages, see John Garth's essay on Tolkien and Longfellow, 'The road from adaptation to invention' in *Tolkien Studies* Vol. XI, pp. 1–44.

L[ongfellow]'s names are often too good to be inventions. See Garth's essay (cited above) for an extended discussion of the relationship among the names in *Kalevala*, 'Hiawatha', and Tolkien's Qenya/Quenya.

the Kal[evala]'s first rush into translations in Scandinavian and German. There was indeed a 'rush into translations' starting with a translation into Swedish of the Old (1835) *Kalevala* by Matthias Castrén (a Finn) in 1841. In 1845 Jakob Grimm included thirty-eight lines from Runo 19 in a presentation to the German Academy of Sciences, and a complete translation into German of the New (1849) *Kalevala* was produced by Anton Schiefner in 1852.

'Chanting the Hundredth Psalm that Grand old Puritan Anthem'. Tolkien's syntax makes it hard to figure out exactly who said what to whom about what, but apparently it is an 'American appreciation' quoted in the *London Daily News* as praising Longfellow's 'The Courtship of Miles Standish' for containing 'one of the most marvellous lines in all English.' The line in question (misquoted in Tolkien's text) describes

Priscilla Mullens, the object of the Courtship, 'singing the hundredth Psalm, the grand old Puritan anthem'. Equally unclear is the object of Tolkien's obvious sarcasm, whether it is the American appreciator of the quote, the *London Daily News* for its taste in poetry, or Longfellow for calling a Hebrew Psalm a 'Puritan anthem'. Or all of these.

79 **Ilmarinen.** One of the 'big three' heroes of *Kalevala*. His name is formed from *ilma*, 'sky', with the occupational suffix *ri*. He has the epithets *seppo*, 'craftsman', and *takoja*, 'hammerer, forger'. He was originally the maker of the sky, Finnish *kirjokansi* the 'decorated/many-coloured lid', and is the forger of the Sampo, the mysterious creation which is the object of contention in *Kalevala*.

Kaukomieli. A by-name or epithet for Lemminkainen, the reckless playboy, third of the 'Big Three'. Magoun translates Kaukomieli as 'man with a far-roving mind'; Friburg as 'far-minded', Kuusi, Bosley and Branch as 'far-sighted' or 'proud'.

80 **'speeches in part'.** A convention of folk tale and folk poetry in which inanimate but personified objects have voices and speak for themselves, usually to or about human characters. The harp in 'Jack and the Beanstalk' telling the giant that Jack is stealing it is an example. Tolkien used the convention in *The Hobbit* when he had the Trolls' purse speak to Bilbo, who was trying to steal it.

82 **Ahti and his wife Vellamo dwell in the waters.** Ahti appears most often as a by-name for Lemminkainen, while Kirby

gives Ahto as the name of the God of the Sea and of the Waters, husband of Vellamo, according to Kirby 'the goddess of the Sea and of the Waters, the spouse of Ahto.' Ahti as a variant of Ahto does, however, occasionally appear as the name of a water-god.

The Kalevala

[*Typescript draft*]

I am afraid this paper was not originally written for this society, which I hope it will pardon since I produce it mainly to form a stop-gap to night, and to entertain you as far as possible in spite of the sudden collapse of the proper speaker. I hope you will also forgive, besides its second-hand character its quality – which is hardly that of a paper, rather a disconnected soliloquy accompanied by a leisurely patting on the back of a pet volume. If I continually drop into talking of these poems as if no one in the room had ever heard of them but myself, you must attribute it to the strange chance that no one had when I read the paper before; and you must also attribute it to the 'pet'-attitude. I am very fond of these poems – they are literature so very unlike any of the things that are familiar to general readers, or even to those who stray in the more curious by-paths – they are so very un-European, and yet could only come from Europe.

Anyone who has read the collection of ballads which go by this name (more especially if he has read them, or even part of them, in the original – a vastly different thing to any translation) will I think agree to that. Most people are familiar from the days of their earliest books onwards with the general mould and type of mythological stories; legends, tales, romances, and so on, that come to us by many and crooked channels from ancient Hellas and the southern lands, from the North and the grim Germanic peoples, from the islands of the West and their old Keltic lords (whatever Keltic may mean). For some of us, for more than are often willing or honest enough to confess it, these achieved their crowning glory and delight in Stead's pink-covered Books for the Bairns – that mine of ancient and undying lore. They have a certain style, or savour; a something akin to one another in them, in spite of their vast cleavages; a something that is more than the universal community of human imagination, and that makes you feel that, whatever the ultimate differences of race of those speakers, there is something kindred in the imagination of the speakers of Indo-european languages. Some far off things there were, of course, even in those little pink books; echoes from the black heart of Africa; trickles from a distant and alien East. Nothing in this world can be finally defined, or marked out with rigid lines. So it is with Europe. It has south-eastern frontiers over which have perpetually poured the influences, half-asiatic, half close kindred to ourselves, of the Semitic languages and cultures to be assimilated swiftly and often beyond easy recognition in Europe. But that is an old tale; and even perhaps while we are still arguing whether the Far East has given us more than a plot here, the shadow of an old tale there to be turned to our own uses, you come one very fine day upon the Kalevala, the Land of Heroes. Then you are indeed in a quite new world and can revel in an amazing new excitement.

We will avoid the Peak in Darien, if only for the reason that I at any rate am not remaining silent about/upon it – still you do feel like a Columbus landing on a new continent, a Thorfinn Karlsefni in a Vinland the Good – and better off, for your new heroic acquaintances are better fun than Skraeling or Red Indian. Of course when you first step onto the new ground you can, if you like, at once begin comparing it with the places you have come from. There are mountains, rivers, grass, and other things here much as the[re] were there; many plants and some animals (especially the ferocious human species) may seem familiar – but it is more than likely that an indefinable sense of newness will either delight or disturb you too much for comparisons, there will be a glamour of strangeness even upon the familiar things; the trees will group themselves unusually on the horizon; the birds will make unfamiliar music; the inhabitants will talk a wild and at first unintelligible lingo. After the country and its manners have become better known to you, and you have got on speaking terms with the natives, you will, I hope, find it jolly to live awhile with this strange people and these new gods, with this race of unhypocritical low-brow scandalous heroes, and sadly unsentimental lovers – some there may be who will think with regret that they have ever to go back from that land at all. There are possibly some, however, that I have not yet considered, people of irreproachable education and faultless urbanity who would desire only to catch the first liner back to their familiar cities. These people had better be off soon. I have no defence to offer them for the 'Land' or its 'Heroes'; for to them it is useless to say that, if the heroes of the Kalevala do behave with a singular lack of dignity and even decency, and with a readiness for tears and dirty dealing, that is part of their especial attraction! After all they are not really more undignified – and are much more easy to get on with – than is a medieval lover who takes to his bed to lament the cruelty of his lady in that she will not have pity on him, condemning him to a melting death; but who is struck with the novelty of the idea when his kindly adviser points out that the poor lady is as yet uninformed in any way of his attachment. The lovers of Kalevala are forward and take a deal of rebuffing. There is no Troilus to need a Pandarus to do his shy wooing for him; rather here it is the mothers-in-law who do some sound bargaining behind the scenes, and give cynical advice to their daughters calculated to shatter the stoutest illusions.

Wonder and a little bewilderment were at any rate my experience when I first came upon the Kalevala – crossed, that is, the gulf between the Indo-european-speaking peoples of Europe into the smaller realm of those who still cling in queer corners to half-forgotten tongues and memories of an elder day. The newness worried me, sticking in awkward lumps through the clumsiness of a translation that had not overcome all the peculiar difficulties of its task; it irritated while it attracted – but the more I read of it, the more I felt at home and enjoyed myself. Then I made a wild assault on the original language, and was at first repulsed with heavy losses, and can never be said to have taken the position. Still it is easy to see why translations are not very good, or very near to their original – they are dealing with a language separated by an immeasurable gulf in nature and in method of expression from English. Finnish is an odd tongue, very fitting to the 'Land of Heroes' (as is natural), and as different from anything that you are familiar with as the tales of these poems are from the tales you knew before.

One repeatedly hears the 'Land of Heroes' described as the Finnish National Epic – as if it was of the nature of the universe that every nation (dreary word), besides a national bank, and government, should before qualifying for membership of the League, show lawful possession also of a National Epic, hall-remark of respectability, evidence indeed of national existence. But Finland does not possess one. The Kalevala certainly is not one. It is a mass of conceivably epic material (I can conceive of the epic that should grow from it with difficulty, I must confess); but – and I think this is the main point – it would lose all that is its greatest delight, if ever it were one unhappy day to be epically handled. The mere stories, bare events, alone could remain; all that undergrowth, that rich profusion and luxuriance, which clothe them would have to be stripped away. Indeed, the 'Land of Heroes' is a collection of exactly that absorbingly delightful material which on the appearance of an epic artist, and of an age lofty-minded enough to produce him, has elsewhere inevitably been cast aside, and fallen at last out of even 'oral literature' into disuse and final oblivion. Barely in the Kalevala do passages or episodes appear that one can conceive of as capable of being tuned to the higher emotional pitches required by the greater poetry. It is to all that body of strange myth, of queer troglodyte underworld of story, of wild jugglings with the sun and moon and the origins of the earth and the shapes of Man, that in Homer (for instance) has lightly been pruned away till only a few incongruous traces of its former presence are left – it is to this that most of the Kalevala may be compared and not to the large grandeur of the epic theme, nor to its conscious humanity. Or again it is to the weird tales, the outrageous ghosts, and the sorceries and by-tracks of Northern imagination that crop out at times into the usually intensely clear upper air of the Sagas that the Land of Heroes can most often be likened, not to the haughty dignity and courage, the nobility of mind and of body of which the great Sagas tell. Yet the queer and strange, the unrestrained, the grotesque is not only interesting it is valuable: it is one of the eternal and permanent interests and attractions of men. Nor is it always necessary to purge it all out in order to attain to the sublime. You can have your gargoyles on your noble cathedral; but northern Europe has lost much through too often trying to build Greek temples. Tonight I am not in the least concerned however even to be sublime – I am content to turn over the pages of these mythological ballads – full of that very primitive undergrowth that the literature of Europe has on the whole been steadily cutting away and reducing for many centuries with different and earlier completeness among different people[.] I would that we had more of it left – something of the same sort that belonged to the English – but my desire is not due to one very dreadful and fatal motive; it is not adulterated with science; it is clear of all suspicion of Anthropology. Any such collection as this would be, and indeed I am only too well aware is, the playground of anthropologists and comparative mythologists, where they luxuriate mightily awhile – but however good and interesting in its own way their sport and hunting may be (I fear I am often sceptical) it is as foreign to my present purpose as would be the processes of the manufacture of cheese. Commentators, I know, make many notes to these poems such as: 'compare this story with the one told in the Andaman Isles', or 'compare that belief with the one mentioned in the Hausa folk-tales', and so forth – but don't let us. These notes seldom prove anything more than that Finns and Andaman Islanders are though rather different to look at nearly related animals, and that we knew before. Let us rather be glad that we have come suddenly upon a storehouse of those popular imaginings that we had feared lost, stocked with stories not yet sophisticated into a sense of proportion, with no thought of the decent limits even of exaggeration, with no sense (or certainly not our sense) of the incongruous, unless, as we may at times suspect, incongruity is delighted in. We are taking a holiday from the whole course of European progress of the last three millenniums, and going to be wildly un-hellenic and barbarous for a time – like the boy who hoped that the future life would provide for half-holidays in Hell far away from Eton collars and hymns. For the moment we are not to apply our superior modern intellect to the analysing of these things. We should rather try to enter into their especial spirit on terms of equality. The vivisectionist is able to make a case out for himself, but no one believes that he knows more about dogs than the man that keeps them as pets – but even the superiority that enters into the word pet should be got rid of – I should have said who makes a companion of a dog. The only analysis I have allowed myself is a gentle probing into my own feelings of pleasure into the savour perceived in these poems; some little effort to describe the life, the landscape and the people of this land as they presented themselves to me.

The delicious exaggerations of these wild tales could no doubt be learnedly compared to a hundred primitive or modern uncivilized literatures, and collections of legend – but, even if I could, I wouldn't for the present move outside Europe; for however wild, uncivilized and primitive these things may be their atmosphere and landscape belong essentially to Northern Europe, and to emphasize that I would willingly forgo a hundred parallelisms. It is all the same true that the unrestraint and exaggeration in the

Kalevala does at once recall such things as say the Welsh stories of the Mabinogion, and other similar things in Welsh and Irish; but in reality their cases are very different. In the Kalevala there is often no attempt at even the limited plausibility of the fairy-tale, no cunning concealment of the impossible – only the child's delight in saying that he has cut down a million trees, or that he will knock down some such august personage as his father, if indeed he has not already slain twenty policemen. All this is not intended to take you in, nor even to cast the brief spell of the story-teller's illusion over you. Its delight depends on the dawning perception of the limits of ordinary human possibility and at the same time of the limitless power of movement and of creation of the human fancy and imagination. Latent in it no doubt is the heroism of the human battles with overmastering fate, and courage undaunted by unconquerable odds – but you do not listen to it on that account, you either like it or despise it as an effort of fresh unsophisticated fancy. Of course in the Welsh tales there is often, indeed continually, in evidence the same delight in a picturesque lie, in a strong breathless flight of fancy; but paradoxically the Welsh tales are both far more absurd and far less so than the Finnish. They are more absurd for they are (when we get them) less fresh than they once were; there is in many places a thick dust of a no longer understood tradition lying on them; strings of names and allusions that no longer have any meaning, that were already nonsense for the bards who related them. Any one who wants to see what I mean has only to look at the catalogue of the heroes of Arthur's court in the story of Kilhwch and Olwen, or the account of the feats that Kilhwch had to perform for the giant Yspaddaden Penkawr in order to win his daughter Olwen. There is little or nothing of this strange lumber in the Kalevala. On the other hand, the Welsh stories are far less absurd for the pictures painted have far more technique; their colours are cleverly, even marvellously schemed; their figures are cunningly grouped. The fairy-tale's own plausibility is respected; if a man slays an impossible monster, the story holds firm to its lie. In the Land of Heroes a man may kill a gigantic elk in one line and find it more poetic to call it a she-bear in the next. To elaborate this is perhaps unnecessary; but it might be made the occasion of an attempt to say just what I find the atmosphere of the Kalevala to be – my finding you can correct for yourselves from your own knowledge, or from the extracts that I could wish to read to you until your patience was exhausted, and you felt the appropriateness of the last lines of the Kalevala:

'Een the waterfall when flowing
Yields no endless stream of water;
Nor does an accomplished singer
Sing till all his knowledge fail him.'

It seems to me that what one feels immediately is that there is no background of literary or artistic tradition. The Mabinogion, for instance, has such a background; it is full of the sense of long years of development and even of decay which has resulted, on the one hand, in the cumbering of the tale with forgotten traditional names and matter, and on the other has produced a field of the most excellently harmonised and subtly varied colours against which the figures of the actors stand out – but they also harmonise with the marvellous surrounding colour-scheme and lose in startlingness if not in clearness. If few have the same intensely vivid feeling for colour that Keltic tales show, yet most similar national legendary literatures have something of this – the Kalevala to me feels to have none. The colours, the deeds, the marvels, the figures of the heroes are all splashed onto a clean bare canvas by a sudden hand; even the legends concerning the origin of the most ancient things in the world seem to come fresh from the singer's hot imagination of the moment. Certainly there are no modernities in it like trams or guns or aeroplanes; the heroes' weapons it is true are the so-called antique bow and spear and sword, but at the same time there is a 'nowness', a quite unhazy unromantic momentariness and presentness that startles you mightily when you suddenly realize that you are all the time reading about the earth being made out of a teal's egg, or of the sun and moon being imprisoned in a mountain. All things must be bought at a price and we have purchased the comparat[ive]-consistency and reasonableness of our tales, the clearer crystallisation of our traditions with the loss of this magic and untarnished freshness.

Now as to what is known of the origin of these poems I know little and will not try to tell much more tha[n] I know. Ever since the coming of Väinämöinen and the making of his great harp, the 'kantele' fashioned of pike-bone, from what we know of the Finns they have always loved ballads of this sort; and ballads of this sort have been handed on and sung day after day with unending zest from father to son, and from son to grandson down to the present day, when, as the ballads now lament, 'the songs are songs of bygone ages, hidden words of ancient wisdom, songs which all the children sing not, all beyond men's comprehension'. The shadow of Sweden and then of Russia has been over the country for many centuries. Petrograd is in Finland. Things are not, it is to be feared, much better now. The remarkable and delightful thing for us, however, is that these 'songs of bygone ages' have somehow been preserved without being tinkered with. Sweden finally in the 12th century conquered Finland (or rather the Finns – their land has never had the hard and fast boundaries of the modern European states). Before that there was continual warfare and continual intercourse with the Northerly Germanic peoples that stretches back beyond the beginnings of our era, and in which doubtless the first bearers of the English name in Holstein and the Islands had a good part – but the intercourse goes back even earlier than that far time. By the Swedish conquest, and by the swords of the Teutonic Knights Christianity began slowly to be introduced – in other words the Finns were one of the last acknowledged pagan peoples of Mediaeval Europe. Today the Kalevala and its themes are still practically untouched by this influence, much less affected by it than the mythology of ancient Scandinavia as it appears in the Edda. Except in the story of the virgin Marjatta at the end, in a few references to Jumala or Ukko god of the Heavens, and so forth, even hints at the existence of Christianity are almost entirely absent; of its spirit there is nothing, as any one can see who compares the crude story of Marjatta with Christian faith. To this is of course largely ascribable the interesting primitiveness of the poems, the 'undergrowth' character of them, though it is also partly responsible for their minor emotional key, their narrow and parochial view – things that in our present holiday mood are not without attraction. For another seven centuries the ballads have been sung in spite of Sweden, in spite of Russia, and do not ever appear to have been written down at all till Elias Lönnrot in 1835 made a collection of many of them, and published a selection of these. These were all collected in Eastern Finland and are consequently in a dialect differ- ent from that that has since come to be the modern literary dialect of Finnish. This Kalevala dialect has come now to be a kind of poetic convention. Lönnröt was not the only collector, but it was to him that it occurred to string a selection into a loosely connected form – as it would seem from the result with no small skill. He it was who called this string the Land of Heroes, or Kalevala from Kaleva the mythological ancestor of all the heroes. It consisted of 25 runos or cantos. This was enlarged with freshly collected material to double the size and published again in 1849, and almost immediately appeared in translations.

With regard to what I have said above it is however well to remember that apart from selection and arrangement these things were taken down straight from the lips of

Finnish minstrels, and that the collection did not kill the minstrelsy; the ballad-singing still goes on (or did until the late war); those ballads here by chance crystallized for us are capable of, and still undergo, a thousand variations. The Kalevala too is by no means all the ballad-literature of Finland; it is not even the whole of the collections of Lönnröt alone, who published as well another whole volume of them under the name of 'Kanteletar' the Daughter of the Harp. The Kalevala is only different in that it is more connected and so more readable, and it covers most of the field of Finnish mythology from the Genesis of Earth and Sky to the departure of Väinämöinen. The lateness of the date of the collection and publication is apt to make those with the (probably not entirely wholesome) modern thirst for the 'authentically primitive' doubt whether the wares are quite genuine. Read and doubt no more. Bogus archaism and the pseudo-primitive is as different from this as Ossian is from Middle Irish romance; and anyway the external evidence for the genuineness of these goods is more than sufficient. Indeed the lateness of the collection is very likely the actual reason why the treasure-house has remained unrifled; why its empty shell has not then been whitewashed, redecorated, upholstered in the eighteenth century manner, or otherwise destroyed. It has been left unnoticed to the care of chance, and to the genius of hard-worked uneducated men at the fireside, and has escaped the pedant and the instructive person. More remarkable still, even when collected and suffering at last the fate of reproduction in print, these poems have by luck escaped being roughly or moralistically handled. They have not been twisted into any shape of edification, and remain a very startling sort of reading to be so popular with those now most law-abiding and Lutheran of European peoples, the modern educated Finns. Something of a parallel can be found in the interest of mediaeval Icelandic priests and bishops in the fierce deeds of the pre-christian [*sic*] Scandinavians, and in the often scandalous adventures of Thórr and Ódinn. As a matter of fact one does sometimes hear the Kalevala, and things like it, cited as evidence of the enduring paganism of Europe that (we are told) is still fighting a gallant and holy battle against the oppression of Christianity, and of Hebraic Biblicality. To argue about this would really be to stray far from my present point and purpose; but the temptation to say something about our attitude towards the ancient gods is too strong. Without disputing about the attitude of the Finnish people up to, say, about a century ago when these things were taken down (for I do not know enough about them), I am still quite ready to admit that without something approaching to an objective belief in the old gods we definitely lose something of the magic of all old tales, something in them is 'all beyond our comprehension'; it is no good saying that the sea is still poetically boundless, for to the very people who can appreciate the poetry of the sea the roundness of the earth and the unfortunate existence of America on the other side of a strictly limited Atlantic ocean is most constantly and vividly present in the imagination; the heavenly bodies are by them above all most clearly realized not to be the heavenly beings. The organization and greater security of modern life: gentler social manners; a wealth of bodily conveniences, and comforts, and even destructive luxuries; tobacco, doctors, and police; and more (the one thing that is certainly worth it) freedom from the shadow of the darker crueller and fouler superstitions, we have purchased at a price – there are no magic islands in our Western sea and (as Francis Thompson says) 'none will again behold Apollo in the forefront of the morning, or see Aphrodite in the upper air loose the long lustre of her golden locks'. We are grown older and must face the fact. The poetry of these old things remains being immortal, but no longer for us is the intoxication of both poetry and belief. The holiday I suggested is a holiday from poetic and literary development, from the long accumulated weight of civilised tradition and knowledge, not a decadent and retrograde movement, not a 'nostalgie de la boue' – only a holiday; and if while on this holiday we half hear the voice of Ahti in the noises of the sea, half shudder at the thought of Pohja, gloomy land of witchcraft, or Tuonela yet darker region of the dead, it is nonetheless with quite another part of our minds that we do this than that which we reserve for our real beliefs and for our religion, just as it undoubtedly was for the Icelandic ecclesiastics of old. Yet there may be some whom these old songs will stir to new poetry, just as the old songs of other pagan days have stirred other Christians; for it is true that only the Christians have made Aphrodite utterly beautiful, a wonder for the soul; the Christian poets or those who while renouncing their

Christianity owe to it all their feeling and their art have fashioned nymphs and dryads of which not even Greek ever dreamt; the real glory of Latmos was made by Keats. [*The following sentence is handwritten in ink.*] As the world grows older there is loss and gain – let us not with modern insolence and blindness imagine it all gain (lest this happen such songs as the 'Land of Heroes' are left for our disillusionment); but neither must we with neo-pagan obscurity of thought imagine it all loss.

Returning from my unwarranted digression, I feel that I can not proceed any further without saying something about the language of the poems. Finnish is, for Englishmen at any rate, near the top of the list of the very difficult languages of Europe; though it is anything but ugly. Indeed it suffers like many languages of its type from an excess of euphony; so much so that the music of the language is liable to be expended automatically, and leave over no excess with which to heighten the emotion of a lyric passage. Where vowel-harmony, and the assimilation and softening of consonants is an integral part of ordinary grammar and of everyday speech there is much less chance for sudden unexpected sweetnesses. It is a language practically isolated in modern Europe, except for the language of the Esthonians which is closely akin, as are their tales and their blood. Finno-Ugrian philology, which is no concern of ours now, discovers relationships with tribal non-Russian speeches in modern Russia, and in the far distance (though here it is rather a relationship of type than an ultimate kinship of descent) with the Magyar in Hungary, and further still with

Turkish. It has no kinship at all with either its immediate Germanic or Slavonic neighbours, except in a process of agelong borrowing that has filled it to the brim with old Slavonic, Lithuanian, and Germanic words, many of which preserve in their new soil the form that they have lost centuries ago in their own tongues – such, for instance, is the case with the Finnish word 'kuningas' king which is exactly the form that philologists had assumed that our word 'king' possessed two thousand years ago or thereabouts. In spite of all this borrowing, and the constant cultural influence of the Indo-european neighbouring languages which has left definite traces, Finnish still remains a language far more primitive (and therefore contrary to the usual superstition far more complicated) than most of the other languages in Europe. It still preserves a flexible fluid unfixed state inconceivable even in the most primitive patois of English. There is no need to search for a more startling example of this than the way in which in the poetry meaningless syllables and even meaningless words that merely sound jolly are freely inserted. For instance in such lines as the following:-

'Enkä lähe Inkerelle
Penkerelle Pänkerelle' – or

'Ihveniä ahvenia
Tuimenia taimenia'

'Pänkerelle' merely echoes 'Penkerelle'; 'Ihveniä' and 'tuimenia' are merely invented to set off 'ahvenia' and 'taimenia'. I don't mean to say that this sort of thing is done

often enough to reduce the songs to nonsense rhymes with
flickers of sense; but the mere fact that such things are possible at all even if it may be for special effect or emphasis
is sufficiently astonishing. The metre employed is roughly
the same as that of the translations though much freer
and less monotonous than the English would lead one to
think. It is the octosyllabic line with roughly four beats
or stresses, the rhythm is uniformly trochaic, no upbeat
being used, and there is no rhyme. Two of the stresses
or beats (usually the first and third) tend to stand out as
the most important. It is of course, as far as English can
be made to yield the same effect as Finnish, the metre of
'Hiawatha'. What however is not so generally known is that
not only the metre, but the idea of the poem, and much
too of the matter and incident, was pirated for 'Hiawatha'
– 'Hiawatha' is in fact the first literary offspring of the
Kalevala, and nothing could better emphasize or illustrate
my earlier remarks on the spirit and nature of Finnish
songs than a comparison with their civilized descendant.
'Hiawatha' is not a genuine storehouse of Indian folklore,
but a mild and gentle bowdlerizing of the Kalevala coloured
with disconnected bits of Indian lore, and I imagine a few
genuine legendary names – some of Longfellow's names
sound altogether too good to be invented. It was either
Longfellow's second or third journey to Europe (the one
that had for its object the learning of Danish and Swedish
– Longfellow was a professor of Modern languages) that
coincided with the Kalevala's first rush into Scandinavian
and German translations.

The pathos alone, I think, of the Kalevala finds anything like an equal reflection in the work of its imitator – a mild and rather dull American don, the author of 'Evangeline', who, 'the 'London Daily News' (I am quoting now an old American appreciation) admitted had produced one of the most marvellous lines in all English: 'chanting the Hundredth Psalm, that grand old Puritan anthem." This metre, monotonous and thin as it can be (especially in English), is indeed if well handled capable of the most poignant pathos, if not of more majestic things. I don't mean only the 'Death of Minnehaha', but the 'Fate of Aino' in the Kalevala and the 'Death of Kullervo', where this pathos is enhanced not hindered by the (to us) almost humorous naiveté of the mythological and fabulous surroundings. Pathos is common in the Kalevala and often very true and keen. One of the favourite subjects – not a majestic one, but very well handled – is that other side to a wedding that the 'happy-ever-after' type of literature usually avoids: the lament and heart-sinking of even a willing bride on leaving her father's house and the familiar things of the home. This farewell in the state of society reflected in the Kalevala was evidently often near to tragedy, where mothers-in-law were worse than anywhere else in literature, and where families dwelt in ancestral homes for generations, sons and their wives all under the iron hand of the Matriarch.

If, however, pathos or not, you are bored by the interminable sing-song character of this metre, it is well to remember again that these are only, as it were, accidentally written things – they are in essence song-songs, sing-songs

chanted to the monotonous repetition of a phrase thrummed
on the harp while the singers swayed backwards and
forwards in time.

> 'Let us clasp our hands together,
> Let us interlock our fingers,
> Let us sing a cheerful measure,
> Let us use our best endeavours,
>
> . . . .
>
> And recall our songs and legends
> Of the belt of Väinämöinen,
> Of the forge of Ilmarinen,
> And of Kaukomieli's sword-point.'

So opens the Kalevala, and there are many other references to the rhythmic swaying of the monotonous chanters:
I wish I had ever heard them with my own ears, but I have
not.

The religion of the poems – after headings such as
'language' and 'metre' one feels bound to have another on
'religion' – if indeed such a name can be applied to it, is
a luxuriant animism; it cannot really be separated from
the purely mythological elements. This means that in the
Kalevala every stock and every stone, every tree, the birds,
waves, hills, air, the tables, the swords, and even the beer
have well-defined personalities, which it is often the quaint
merit of these poems to bring out with singular skill and
aptness in numerous speeches in part. One of the most
remarkable of these is the speech of his sword to Kullervo
just before he throws himself upon its point. If a sword

had a character, you feel it would be just such as is pictured there – a cruel and cynical ruffian. There is also, to mention only a few other cases, the lament of the Birch Tree, or the passage (of which the similar passage in Hiawatha is an imitation that does not improve upon its model) where Väinämöinen seeks a tree to give him timber for his boat (Runo XVI); or where Lemminkainen's mother seeking for her lost son asks all things that she meets for news, the moon, the trees, even the pathway – and they all answer in characterised parts. (Runo XV). This indeed is one of the essential features of the songs: even ale talks on occasions – as in a passage that I hope to have time to read, the story of the Origin of Beer. Here is a bit of it (Runo XX 522–556).

'. . . now the bread they baked was ready, and were
    stirred the pots of porridge,
and a little time passed over, when the ale worked in
    the barrels,
and the beer foamed in the cellars:– 'now must some
    one come to drink me,
now must some one come to taste me, that my fame
    may be reported,
and that they may sing my praises.' Then they went to
    seek a minstrel,
went to seek a famous singer, one whose voice was of the
    strongest,
one who knew the finest legends. First to sing they tried
    a salmon,

if the voice of trout was strongest. Singing is not work
    for salmon,
and the pike recites no legends. Crooked are the jaws of
    salmon,
and the teeth of pike spread widely. Yet again they sought
    a singer,
went to seek a famous singer, one whose voice was of the
    strongest,
one who knew the finest legends – and they took a child
    for singer,
thought a boy might sing the strongest. Singing is not
    work for children,
nor are splutterers fit for shouting. Crooked are the
    tongues of children,
and the roots thereof are crooked. Then the red ale grew
    indignant,
and the fresh drink fell to cursing, pent within the oaken
    barrels,
and behind the taps of copper. 'If you do not find a
    minstrel,
do not find a famous singer, one whose voice is of the
    strongest,
one who knows the finest legends, then the hoops I'll burst
    asunder,
and among the dust will trickle . . . .'

Here we hear not only beer speaking and get a hint at
its own estimate of itself as an inspiration of poesy and
song, but we hear the Finnish minstrel cracking up his own

profession, if with greater quaintness, with greater cunning and subtlety than was normally used by the minstrel of mediaeval England and France in similar passages of advertisement. In the Kalevala Beer is the cause of much enthusiasm, but the oft-repeated 'ale is of the finest, best of drinks for prudent people' implies (as do the rest of the poems) a certain moderation in the use of good things. The joys of drunkenness at any rate do not seem to have the same appeal as other vices, though good drink's value in setting free the imagination (and the tongue) was often praised (R. XXI 260).

> '. . . O thou ale thou drink delicious, let the drinkers be
>   not moody.
> Urge the people on to singing; let them shout with mouth
>   all golden,
> till our lords shall wonder at it, and our ladies ponder
>   o'er it.
> For the songs already falter, and the joyous tongues are
>   silenced,
> when the ale is ill-concocted, and bad drink is set before
>   us;
> then the minstrels fail in singing and the best of songs they
>   sing not,
> and our cherished guests are silent, and the cuckoo calls no
>   longer . . .'

Beyond all this personification however there is a wealth of mythology. Every tree, wave, and hill has its nymph and spirit, distinct from the character, apparently, of each

individual object. There is the nymph of the Blood and the
Veins; the spirit of the rudder; there is the moon and his
children, and the Sun and his (they are both masculine);
there is a dim and awesome figure, the nearest approach
to regal dignity in the poems, Tapio, God of the Forest,
and his spouse Mielikki, and their fairy-like son and daughter Tellervo, 'little maiden of the forest clad in soft and
beauteous garments', and her brother Nyyrikki with his red
cap and blue coat; there is Jumala in the heavens (Jumala
whose name is used for God in the Bible, but who in the
poems is usually a god of the air and clouds); and there is
Tuoni in the earth, or rather in some vague dismal region
beside a river of strange things. Ahti and his wife Vellamo
dwell in the waters, and there are a thousand other new
and strange characters for acquaintance – Pakkanen the
Frost; Lempo the spirit of Evil; Kankahatar, the goddess
of weaving – but a catalogue does not inspire those that
have not yet been introduced, and bores those that have.
The division between the offspring of the nymphs, sprites,
and other beings (you can seldom call them Gods – it is
much too Olympian) and the human characters is hardly
drawn at all. Väinämöinen, most venerable of evergreen
patriarchs, mightiest of culture-heroes (he is the God of
Music in Esthonia), most human of liars, is the son of
the Wind and of Ilmatar, daughter of the Air; Kullervo,
most tragic of peasant-boys, is but two generations from
a swan.

I give you just this jumble of gods great and small to
give you some impression of the delightful variety of the

Land of Heroes. If you are not of the temper, or think you are not, for getting on with these divine and heroic personages, I assure you, as I did before, that they behave most charmingly: they all obey the great rule of the game in the Kalevala, which is to tell at least three lies before imparting accurate information, however trivial. It seems to have become a formula or polite behaviour, for no one in the Kalevala is believed until his fourth statement (which he modestly prefaces with 'all the truth I now will tell you, though at first I lied a little'.) So much for the religion (if you can call it such) and the imaginary background.

The real scenery of the poems, the place of most of the action is Suomi, the Marshland – Finland as we call it – which the Finns themselves often name the Land of Ten Thousand Lakes. Short of going there, I imagine one could scarcely be made to see the land more vividly than by reading the Kalevala – the land of a century ago or more, at any rate, if not a land ravaged by modern progress. The poems are instinct with the love of it, of its bogs and wide marshes in which stand islands as it were formed by rising ground and sometimes topped with trees. The bogs are always with you – and a worsted or outwitted hero is invariably thrown into one. One sees the lakes and reed-fenced flats with slow rivers; the perpetual fishing; the pile-built houses – and then in winter the land covered with sleighs, and men faring over quick and firm alike on snow-shoes. Juniper, Pine, fir, aspen, birch are continually mentioned, rarely the oak, very seldom any other tree; and whatever they be nowadays in Finland the bear and wolf are in the Kalevala persons of great importance, and many sub-arctic animals figure in it too, that we do not know in England. The customs are all strange and so are the colours of everyday life; the pleasures and the dangers are

[The typescript stops here in mid-phrase on the last line of the page. The final two words, 'dangers are', are jammed in just beneath and partially overlapping the line above them, as if the paper had unexpectedly run out before the writer stopped typing. A handwritten comment in ink below the text notes: '[Text breaks off here].' What would have been the following page apparently never was typed, but we may conjecture that had it been, it would have conformed more or less to the final page and three quarters of the manuscript draft.]

Notes and Commentary

99 sudden collapse of the proper speaker. That Tolkien was filling in for two collapsed speakers some five to ten years apart, while not impossible, seems to stretch credibility. But since there is no evidence that this version of the talk was ever given, the opening sentence may simply have been transcribed without editing from the earlier version.

literature so very unlike. Note that the word is now spelled with one *t*.

103 taken the position. A military expression, referring to capture of an enemy redoubt, not the assumption of a political or philosophical stance in argument.

104 weird tales. This was the title of an American magazine of pulp fantasy fiction, first published in 1923, but not widely circulated in England. Tolkien's allusion (if such it is) is likelier to have been to E.T.A. Hoffmann's collection of stories, *Weird Tales*, translated from the German by J.T. Bealby and published in England in 1884.

105 **I would that we had more of it left – something of the same sort that belonged to the English.** This statement, misleadingly associated in Humphrey Carpenter's biography with Tolkien's undergraduate time at Oxford, does not appear in the manuscript draft of 1914–15, written while he was still a student and before he went to war. It thus comes out of a different context from the original talk with which Carpenter conflated it, and is all the more to be associated with Tolkien's burgeoning idea of a 'mythology for England'. The remark was Tolkien's response to the myth-and-nationalism movement that spread through Western Europe and the British Isles in the 19th and early 20th centuries but had been brought to a halt by the 1914 war. Out of that pre-war movement came Wilhelm Grimm's *Kinder- und Hausmärchen*, Jacob Grimm's *Deutsche Mythologie*, Jeremiah Curtin's *Myths and Folklore of Ireland*, Moe and Asbjørnsen's *Norske Folkeeventyr*, Lady Guest's translation of the Welsh *Mabinogion*, in addition to Elias Lönnrot's *Old Kalevala* (1835) and expanded *Kalevala* (1849) and a host of other myth and folklore collections.

107 **a no longer understood tradition.** The 19th- and early 20th-century view of Welsh myth as seen in the *Mabinogion* was of a once-coherent concept behind the stories that had been garbled and misunderstood over time, partly through the supervention of Christianity and partly through the limited acquaintance of Christian redactors with the original stories.

108 **the catalogue of the heroes of Arthur's court in the story of Kilhwch and Olwen.** The Arthurian Court List is a 'run' of some 260 names, some historical, some legendary, some alleged to be Arthur's relatives, some obviously fanciful, such as *Clust mab Clustfeinad*, 'Ear son of Hearer' and *Drem mab Dremhidydd*, 'Sight son of Seer'. The recitation would have been a *tour de force* for the bard, as well as an evocation of a host of other untold stories.

    Yspaddaden Penkawr. Yspaddaden 'Chief/Head Giant', is the father of Olwen, Kilhwch's intended bride, and the tasks he assigns are not meant to test the prospective lover but to kill him. The character contributed not a little to Thingol, father of Lúthien, who assigned Beren the task of bringing back a Silmaril from the Iron Crown of Morgoth in the expectation that Beren would die in the attempt.

109 **feeling for colour that Keltic tales show.** The spelling-change from *Celtic* in the manuscript essay to *Keltic* in the typescript revision is noteworthy but absent of explanation. Both spellings are recognized in modern dictionaries, probably due to the word having come into English twice, once through French from Latin and again through German from Greek. The C-spelling comes from the Latin *Celtae* and entered English in the 1600s through French *Celtes*. The K-spelling comes from the original form *Keltoi*, the name given by Greeks to tribes along the Danube and Rhone rivers, and its use by 19th-century German philologists. It has been pointed out to me by Edmund Weiner, co-author with Peter Gilliver and Jeremy Marshall of *The*

Ring of Words: Tolkien and the Oxford English Dictionary, that Tolkien 'was very much in a <k> phase at this time – the Qenya glossary uses <k> throughout, where later he switches to <c> in Elvish' (personal communication).

114 (as Francis Thompson says) 'none will again behold'. Francis Thompson (1859–1907) was an English Catholic poet, best known for 'The Hound of Heaven', which Tolkien admired. The lines quoted here are from the concluding paragraphs of 'Paganism Old and New: The Attempted Revival of the Pagan spirit, with its Tremendous Power of a Past, Though a Dead Past' published in Thompson's collection *A Renegade Poet*. Christopher Tolkien comments in a note in *The Book of Lost Tales, Part One*, that Tolkien 'acquired the Works of Francis Thompson in 1913 and 1914' (*Lost Tales I*, 29).

'nostalgie de la boue'. Literally, 'yearning for the mud'. Metaphorically, the phrase describes the desire, exemplified by the Romantic attraction to the primitive, to ascribe higher spiritual values to people and cultures popularly considered lower than one's own. The attitude was widespread in the late 19th and early 20th centuries, initiated by antiquarians, energized by the discoveries of archaeologists, and fueled by anthropological research into comparative mythology and philology, all of which encouraged the finding of value in the archaic and primitive for its own sake. The word *folklore*, with its condescending assumption that the 'folk' are other (and less educated) than the users of the term, illustrates the mind-set.

the voice of Ahti in the noises of the sea. See the note on 'Ahti' following the manuscript version.

121 Finnish minstrel cracking up his own profession. Talking up his own profession, praising it. Tolkien is using *crack* (derived from Middle English *crak*, 'loud conversation, bragging talk') as a verb in the dialectal expression *to crack up*, meaning 'to praise, eulogize (a person or a thing)'. OED definition 8.

Tolkien, *Kalevala*, and 'The Story of Kullervo'

The Story of Kullervo was an essential step on Tolkien's road from adaptation to invention that resulted in the 'Silmarillion'. It was the forerunner to and inspiration for his tragic epic of Túrin Turambar, one of the three 'Great Tales' of the fictive mythology of Middle-earth. Without the story itself to fit into the sequence, we have had only the beginning (*Kalevala*) and the end (Túrin) of the process, but not the crucial middle portion.

Humphrey Carpenter's declaration in *J.R.R. Tolkien: a biography*, that episodes in Tolkien's tale of Túrin Turambar were 'derived quite consciously from the story of Kullervo in the *Kalevala*' (*J.R.R. Tolkien: a biography*, p. 96), is correct, yet seems in conflict with his judgment in the same paragraph that the influence of *Kalevala* on the Túrin story was 'only superficial' (ibid., p. 96). In fact, this judgment, like Carpenter's misplacement of Tolkien's 'something of the same sort' comment (see note, p. 128), is quite off the mark. Far from being a superficial influence on Túrin, Kullervo's story in *Kalevala* had a profound effect and was the root and source of the story, though filtered through Tolkien's own (at that time unknown) adaptation. Carpenter's biography was published in the same year – 1977 – as Christopher Tolkien's edition of *The Silmarillion*, which gave readers their first look at the saga of Túrin and enabled them to compare it with the Kullervo story in *Kalevala*.

One of the earliest scholars* to seize the opportunity for comparison was Randel Helms, whose 1981 *Tolkien and the Silmarils* suggested that the story in *Kalevala* 'is a tale that begs to be transformed'. But without access to *The Story of Kullervo*, Helms could only see Tolkien 'learning to outgrow an influence, transform a source', from the 'lustful and murderous' Kullervo of *Kalevala* (Helms, p. 6) to the

---

* For a general discussion see Randel Helms, *Tolkien and the Silmarils*. Boston: Houghton Mifflin Company, 1981; J.B. Hines, 'What J.R.R. Tolkien Really Did With the Sampo' *Mythlore* 22.4 (# 86) (200): 69–85; B. Knapp, 'A Jungian Reading of the *Kalevala* 500–1300: Finnish Shamanism – the Patriarchal Senex Figure' Part 1. *Mythlore* 8.3 (# 29) (1981): 25–28; Part 2 'The Archetypal Shaman/Hero' *Mythlore* 8.4 (# 30) (1982), 33–36; Part 3 'The Anima Archetype' *Mythlore* 9.1 (#31) (1982): 35–36; Part 4 'Conclusion' *Mythlore* 9.2 (# 32) (1982): 38–41; Charles E. Noad, 'On the Construction of "The Silmarillion"', and Richard C. West, 'Turin's *Ofermod*', in *Tolkien's Legendarium: Essays on* The History of Middle-earth, ed. Verlyn Flieger and Carl Hostetter, Westport, Connecticut: Greenwood Press, 2000; Tom Shippey, 'Tolkien and the Appeal of the Pagan: *Edda* and *Kalevala*', David Elton Gay, 'J.R.R. Tolkien and the *Kalevala*' and Richard C. West, 'Setting the Rocket off in Story' in *Tolkien and the Invention of Myth*, ed. Jane Chance. Lexington: University Press of Kentucky, 2004; Anne C. Petty, 'Identifying England's Lönnrot' (*Tolkien Studies* I, 2004, 69–84).

lovable but wayward and wrong-headed Túrin Turambar of his own legendarium. Interest in Kullervo as a source thus grew slowly, with the critical commentary of necessity overleaping the unpublished story to jump straight from *Kalevala* to *The Silmarillion*. The predictable result was that even so distinguished a Tolkien scholar as Tom Shippey could concede that 'the basic outline of the tale (of Túrin) owes much to the "Story of Kullervo" in the *Kalevala*' (*The Road to Middle-earth*, p. 297), note the likenesses in ruined family, fosterage, incest with a sister, the conversation with the sword, and stop there.

The pace picked up as the 20th century turned to the 21st. Charles Noad conceded that 'insofar as Kullervo served as the germ for Túrin, this was in one sense the beginning of the *legendarium*, but only as a model for future work' (*Tolkien's Legendarium*, p. 35). Given the lack of additional evidence, that, perforce, was all that scholars could conclude. Richard West, in general agreement with Carpenter and Helms, observed that 'the story of Túrin did not remain a retelling of the story of Kullervo', adding that 'if we had the earliest version we would undoubtedly see that Tolkien started out that way, as he said, but at some point he diverged to tell a new story in the old tradition' (ibid., 238). In her much later article, 'Identifying England's Lönnrot' (*Tolkien Studies* I, 2004, 69–84), Anne Petty compared Tolkien with Elias Lönnrot, the compiler of *Kalevala*, calling attention to the way in which both mythmakers drew on earlier sources in applying their own organization and textualization to the story elements, Lönnrot's sources

being actual rune-singers as well as earlier folklore collectors, and Tolkien's limited (as far as she knew) to the
invented bards, scribes, and translators within his fiction.
What Helms and Shippey and West and Petty lacked
access to was the extra-mythological, transitional story and
transitional character that contributed substantially to the
transformation.

The appearance in 1981 of *The Letters of J.R.R. Tolkien*
gave us more information but little clarification, for the
letters sent mixed signals, or at least showed Tolkien's
mixed feelings about the relative importance of *Kalevala* to
his own mythology. His disclaimer that, as 'The Children
of Húrin', the Kullervo story was 'entirely changed except
in the tragic ending' (*Letters*, p. 345) probably influenced
Carpenter's 'only superficial' comment. But while it is
understandable that Tolkien would want to privilege his
own invention and establish his story's independence from
its source, other more positive references to *Kalevala* in his
letters give a different impression. The mythology 'greatly
affected' him (144); the language was like 'an amazing
wine' (214); 'Finnish nearly ruined [his] Hon. Mods.' (87);
Kalevala 'set the rocket off in story' (214); it was 'the
original germ of the Silmarillion' (87). There is no question
that Túrin Turambar is a fully realized character in his own
right, far richer and better developed than the Kullervo of
Kalevala, and situated in an entirely different context. In
that respect, it could truthfully be said that the story was
'entirely changed'. But an essential step was omitted. The
figure of Kullervo passed through a formative middle stage

between the two. *The Story of Kullervo* is the missing link in the chain of transmission. It is the bridge by which Tolkien crossed from the Land of Heroes to Middle-earth. How he made that crossing, and what he took with him are the subjects of my discussion.

Tolkien first read *Kalevala* in the English translation of W.F. Kirby in 1911 when he was at King Edward's School in Birmingham. Though the work itself made a powerful impression on him, Kirby's translation got a mixed reaction. He referred to it as 'Kirby's poor translation' (*Letters*, p. 214), yet observed that in some respects it was 'funnier than the original' (*Letters*, p. 87). Both opinions may have motivated him to borrow from the Exeter College library in November 1911 a copy of Eliot's *A Finnish Grammar*, an effort to learn enough Finnish to read *Kalevala* in the original. Although both Carpenter (Bodleian Library MS Tolkien B 64/6, folio 1; *Biography*, p. 73) and Scull & Hammond (*Chronology*, p. 55; *Guide*, p. 440) date *The Story of Kullervo* to 1914, according to Tolkien's own account it was some time in 1912 that he began the project. A 1955 letter to W.H. Auden dated his attempt to 'reorganize some of the Kalevala, especially the tale of Kullervo the hapless, into a form of my own' to 'the Honour Mods period . . . . Say 1912 to 1913' (*Letters*, pp. 214–15).

Tolkien's memory for dates is not always fully reliable. Witness his dating of *The Lord of the Rings* to 'the years 1936 to 1949' (*The Lord of the Rings*, Foreword to the Second edition, xv) when *The Hobbit* itself was not published until September of 1937, and *The Lord of the Rings* –

begun as a sequel to and initially called 'the new *Hobbit*' – not launched until December of that year. And the letter to Auden citing 1912 to 1913 was written some forty-three years after the 'period' it referred to. Nevertheless, the two references to 'Hon. Mods.' (Honour Moderations – a set of written papers comprising the first of two examinations taken by a degree candidate) are explicit, and identify a specific phase and time in Tolkien's education. He sat for his Honour Moderations at the end of February 1913 (*Biography*, p. 62). The Hon. Mods. 'period' would thus be the time leading up to that, at the latest January 1913 (during which time he was also re-wooing Edith and persuading her to marry him), and more probably also the later months of the preceding year, 1912. He was also at that time apparently in the early stages of inventing Qenya (Carl Hostetter, personal communication), and some of the story's invented names, imitatively Finnish in shape and phonology, have also a noticeable resemblance to early Qenya vocabulary.

Such a convergence of extracurricular interests – teaching himself Finnish (albeit unsuccessfully), 'reorganizing' the tale of Kullervo, and inventing Qenya – would surely be enough to explain Tolkien's confession in the above-cited letter to Auden that he 'came very near having my exhibition [scholarship] taken off me if not being sent down' (*Letters*, p. 214). Nevertheless, this first practical union of 'lit. and lang.' embodied the principle Tolkien was to spend the rest of his life upholding, his staunchly maintained belief that 'Mythology is language and language is mythology' (*Tolkien On Fairy-Stories*, p. 181), that the two are not opposing poles, but opposite sides of the same coin. This was a period in Tolkien's life rich with discoveries that fuelled and fed each other. Much later he wrote to a reader of *The Lord of the Rings*, 'It was just as the 1914 War burst on me that I made the discovery that "legends" depend on the language to which they belong; but a living language depends equally on the "legends" which it conveys by tradition' (*Letters*, p. 231). In the event, he did pass his Hon. Mods., though with a Second, not the hoped-for First, consequently did not have his exhibition taken off, and thankfully was not sent down, though he was per-suaded to change from Classics to English Language and Literature. And in the long run it was legends and language that triumphed, for *Kalevala* and Finnish generated Qenya and *The Story of Kullervo*, and Tolkien's *Kullervo* led to his Túrin, to the 'Silmarillion', and the 'Silmarillion' led by way of *The Hobbit* to *The Lord of the Rings*.

Humphrey Carpenter's dating of the manuscript to 1914 is probably based on Tolkien's statement in the 1914 letter to Edith that [he was] 'trying to turn one of the stories [of *Kalevala*] – which is really a very great story and most tragic – into a short story somewhat on the lines of Morris' romances with chunks of poetry in between' (*Letters*, p. 7). But the activity of a creative spark is hard to pin down. When and where and how does the impulse to tell a story begin? With an 'I can do that' moment while reading someone else's text? With a mental light-bulb in the middle of the night? A note on the back of an envelope? A sentence scribbled on a napkin? Tolkien recognized the quotidian nature of inspiration, writing years later (1956), 'I think a lot of this kind of work goes on at other (to say lower, deeper, or higher introduces a false gradation) levels, when one is saying how-do-you-do, or even "sleeping"' (*Letters*, p. 231). In the case of *The Story of Kullervo* (unlike the opening of *The Hobbit*, by Tolkien's own account written on the back of an exam) we will probably never know precisely.

Taking some time perhaps late in 1912 as the earliest possible starting date, and Carpenter's 1914 as the *terminus ad quem*, we can see *The Story of Kullervo* as the work of a beginning writer. Whatever Tolkien's immediate intent for the story, and whatever its contribution to his later work, it is best understood in retrospect as a trial piece, that of someone learning his craft and consciously imitating existing material. As Carpenter points out, and as Tolkien was at pains to acknowledge, the style is heavily indebted to William Morris, especially *The House of the Wolfings*, itself a stylistic mixture in which narrative prose gives frequent way to 'chunks' of poetic speech. Like its model, Tolkien's story is deliberately antiquated, filled with poetic inversions – verbs before nouns, and archaisms – *hath* for *has*, *doth* for *does*, 'him thought' instead of 'he thought', 'entreated' in place of 'treated'; as well as increasingly lengthy interpolations of spoken verse by various characters. Much of this style carries over to the earliest stories of Tolkien's own mythology, such as 'The Cottage of Lost Play' in *The Book of Lost Tales, Part Two*, and may well have been an influence on the rhythmic, chanted speech of Tom Bombadil.

When we fit this period into the whole arc of Tolkien's creative life, a pattern emerges of successive stages of development, all of them showing the same interests and methods but each having its own individual character. It is important to our understanding that *The Story of Kullervo* was written by a very young man – twenty or so when he may have started, twenty-two at the most when he broke off; *The Lord of the Rings* by a man in middle life – his forties and fifties; and his last short story, *Smith of Wootton Major* (1964–7) by man in his early seventies. A similar arc of changes over time marks the revisions of the 'Silmarillion' material from the earliest phase of 'The Cottage of Lost Play' to the middle period of 'Akallabêth', 'The Notion Club Papers' and 'The Fall of Númenor' to the late and deeply philosophical meditations of the 'Athrabeth Finrod ah Andreth' and 'Laws and Customs Among the Eldar'.

The Story of Kullervo belongs firmly to the pre-'Silmarillion' period. All the evidence suggests that it was written before Tolkien's service in France in 1916, and three years before the 1917–18 creative burst after his return from France that led to the earliest versions of the Great Tales. Yet though it lacks the markers of 'The Shores of Faëry' or 'The Voyage of Éarendel' – two poems from the same period which Tolkien later flagged as forerunners of his mythology – it should nevertheless be credited as an equally significant precursor of the greater work. Tolkien may not have had the 'Silmarillion' in mind when he wrote *The*

Story of Kullervo, but he certainly had *The Story of Kullervo* in his head when he began the 'Silmarillion'. This early narrative was an essential step in Tolkien's progress as a writer. It contributed substantially to the 1917 'Turambar and the Foalókë' and later versions of that story, as well as to the 1917 'Tale of Tinúviel' and its later versions, for which it somewhat surprisingly provided a significant character. It was a creative pivot, swinging between its *Kalevala* source and the legendarium for which it was itself a source.

But what was it about this particular story that so powerfully called to him that he wrote it not once but several times? Perhaps thinking of its explicitly pagan orientation 'when magic was yet new', John Garth calls it 'a strange story to have captured the imagination of a fervent Catholic' (*Tolkien and the Great War*, p. 26). Tolkien clearly did not find it strange ('great' and 'tragic' were his adjectives), and seems to have felt no conflict with his Catholicism, which at that point was apparently not very 'fervent' anyway. Carpenter cites Tolkien's acknowledgment that his first terms at Oxford 'had passed "with practically none or very little practice of religion"' (*Biography*, p. 58), and notes his 'lapses of the previous year [1912]' (ibid., p. 66). Connecting Tolkien's attraction to the Kullervo story to his guardian-enforced separation from Edith, Garth proposes that its appeal may have lain 'partly in the brew of maverick heroism, young romance, and despair' (*Tolkien and the Great War*, p. 26). Without discounting Garth's connection of the story to Tolkien's immediate situation, it seems possible that the story of Kullervo also resonated deeply with the circumstances of his very early life. Kullervo's description of himself as 'fatherless beneath the heavens' and 'from the first without a mother' (Kirby vol. 2, p. 101, ll. 59–60) cannot be overlooked, still less two cancelled lines of verse, stark and explicit, transferred unchanged from the Kirby *Kalevala* wherein Kullervo bewails his fate to one of the 'chunks of poetry' in Tolkien's own story:

> I was small and lost my ~~mother~~ father
> I was young (weak) and lost my mother.
> (Tolkien MS B 64/6, fol. 11 verso)

The fact that he first included and then crossed out these lines is significant. They may have been at once right on the mark and too close for comfort to the tragedy of his own life. Like Kullervo, Tolkien had lost first his father, and then his mother. When he was small (a child of four) his father died; when he was young (a boy of twelve but surely feeling 'weak' at the loss) his mother died suddenly and unexpectedly, from untreated diabetes.

Let us look at the narrative that Tolkien called 'most tragic'. Strife between brothers leads to the killing of Kullervo's father Kalervo by his uncle Untamo, who lays waste to his family home and abducts Kullervo's unnamed mother, identified in the poem only as 'one girl, and she was pregnant' (Kirby vol. 2, p. 70, l. 71). Kullervo is born into captivity, and as an infant swears revenge on Untamo, who, after three attempts to kill the precocious boy plus the failure to get any work out of him, sells him as a bond-slave to the smith Ilmarinen. The smith's wife sets him to herding the cattle, but cruelly and deliberately bakes a stone into his bread. When he cuts into the bread, his knife, his only memento of his father, strikes the stone and the point breaks. Kullervo's revenge is to enchant bears and wolves into the shape of cows and drive them into the barnyard at milking-time. When the smith's wife tries to milk these bogus cattle they attack and kill her. Kullervo then flees, but being told by the Blue-robed Lady of the Forest that his family is alive, decides to go home, vowing again to kill Untamo. He is deflected from his vengeance by a chance encounter with a girl whom he either seduces or rapes (the story is equivocal on this point). Upon disclosing their parentage to each other, the two discover that they are brother and sister. In despair, the girl throws herself over a waterfall. Consumed with guilt, Kullervo fulfils his vengeance, returning to Untamo's homestead to kill him and burn all his farm buildings, then asks his sword if it will kill him. The sword agrees, and Kullervo finds 'the death he sought for' (Kirby vol. 2, p. 125, l. 341).

I do not propose a one-to-one equation between Kullervo and Tolkien; nor do I claim autobiographical intent on Tolkien's part. Parallels there certainly are, but Father Francis Morgan, Tolkien's guardian, was no murderous Untamo (though he did separate John Ronald from the girl he loved). Beatrice Suffield, the aunt in whose care Tolkien and his brother were temporarily put after their mother died, was not the malicious and sadistic smith's wife –

though Carpenter notes that she was 'deficient in affection' (*Biography*, p. 33). Tolkien was neither a cowherd nor a magician, though he did become a writer of fantasy. Nor did he engage in revenge-killing or commit incest. And though unlike Kullervo he was not mistreated and abused, like Kullervo he was not in control of his own life. There was undeniably something in Kullervo's story which touched him deeply and made him want to 'reorganize [it] into a form of [his] own.' And that something stayed viable as his legendarium took shape.

Garth is right about one thing, however. It is a 'strange story', as even a cursory synopsis shows: a perplexing jumble of loosely connected episodes in which people do inexplicable things for unexplained reasons or for the wrong reason or for no reason at all. With the exception of Kullervo, the characters are one-dimensional – the wicked uncle, the cruel foster-mother, the wronged girl; and Kullervo himself, while more fleshed-out, is an enigma both to himself and to those he meets. The story is not so strange, however, in Tolkien's version, which carefully connects cause, effect, motivation, and outcome. Already a certain modus operandi is in place, the effort to adapt a traditional story to his own liking, to fill in the gaps in an existing story and tidy up the loose ends. The best-known example is *The Hobbit*, in which Bilbo's theft of a cup from the dragon's hoard is a hard-to-miss (for those who've read *Beowulf*) reworking of a problem passage in that poem where, because the manuscript is damaged, the text is full of holes, with words, phrases and whole lines missing or indecipherable, rendering the entire episode an unsolvable puzzle.

In *Beowulf* (lines 2214–2231) an unidentified man driven by unknown necessity creeps into the dragon's lair and steals a cup, which wakens the dragon and leads to the final confrontation that ends in Beowulf's death. Too much is missing for us to know anything more about the circumstances. Though he denied any conscious intent, Tolkien fills in the holes and answers the questions in a major scene in *The Hobbit*. The unknown thief is Bilbo, his necessity is to prove himself as a 'burglar', he steals the cup to demonstrate his prowess to Thorin and the dwarves, and flees up the tunnel, leaving behind him a wrathful Smaug who wreaks vengeance on Lake-town. Tolkien did much the same kind of thing, though more poetically, in his *Sigurd and Gudrún* poems, straightening out the tangle of Old Norse, Icelandic, and Germanic legends that make up the story of Sigurd and the Völsungs (there are, for example – and for unexplained reasons – two Brynhilds, one a valkyrie, the other the very human daughter of King Buthli), and filling in the missing eight pages in the Eddic manuscript (for more on this see Tom Shippey's discussion in his excellent review-article on *The Legend of Sigurd and Gudrún* in *Tolkien Studies*, vol. VII).

Returning now to *Kalevala* and *The Story of Kullervo* let us consider what Tolkien chose to keep, what he left out, what he changed and how he changed it in this earliest attempt at re-writing myth. The major items include:

1. Kullervo's family.
2. His sister.
3. His personality.
4. His dog.
5. His weapons.
6. His incest.
7. His ending.

I'll finish with a brief look (brief because it will be obvious to anyone who has read *The Silmarillion*) at the effect this transitional piece had on his subsequent work, contributing episodes and characters, and deepening the emotional level of his legendarium.

First, Kullervo's family. One of the problem points in the *Kalevala* story is that Kullervo has two families and becomes an orphan twice. His first family is destroyed by Untamo in the raid that captures Kullervo's mother. The narrative is clear at this early point in the story that this is a near-complete massacre, leaving the newborn boy with no home, no father, and no living relatives besides his mother, who like him is a slave and of little help or support. It is thus confusing to most readers when much later in the story a second family in a different household turns up, before the incest but after Kullervo kills the smith's wife. He is at that point told, to his and the reader's surprise, that his family is alive. The thematic justification for this second appearance is that it gives him a set of relatives – another father and a new-found brother and sister – whose job is to tell him in elaborate verse how much they don't care whether he lives or dies, thus reinforcing the feelings of alienation and rejection he's already got from Untamo and the smith's wife. The plot function is to provide Kullervo with a sister that he has never seen and so set the stage for the incest.

According to Domenico Comparetti, one of the earliest scholars to write on *Kalevala*, the two-family mix-up is the result of Lönnrot's combining into one sequence several songs originally independent of one another. Comparetti pointed out that, 'Kullervo's finding his family at home after they have been killed by Untamo, is a contradiction that betrays the joining together of several runes' (Comparetti, p. 148), runos not even from the same localities, and with differing variants (ibid., p. 145). The confusion is not unlike the two Brynhilds mix-up in the Völsung story. Lönnrot may have been juggling his material, but he had precedents. In these earlier versions, the hero's name is not always Kullervo; in Ingria it is Turo or Tuirikkinen, in Archangel and Karelia it is Tuiretuinen (Comparetti, pp. 147–48). There is no hard evidence that Tolkien had read Comparetti, though it seems probable given his fascination with *Kalevala*, and his discussion in the two College talks of the geographical range of Lönnrot's collecting is most likely drawn from Comparetti. But it was the effect of *Kalevala* 'as is,' not its history of composition or its component parts which so engaged Tolkien. His quote from George Dasent that, 'We must be satisfied with the soup that is set before us, and not desire to see the bones of the ox out of which it has been boiled' (*The Monsters and the Critics and Other Essays*, p. 120), was as applicable to Finnish mythology as to fairy-stories.

Tolkien ignored the bones, eliminating the second family altogether and giving the first family those extra children, an older brother and sister already in place before Untamo's raid. Their mother, pregnant again at the time Untamo attacks, gives birth to twins after she is abducted by Untamo. These are a boy whom she names Kullervo, or 'Wrath', and a girl she names Wanōna, or 'Weeping'. The pre- and post-Untamo sets of children are not close in either age or temperament, and the older set is hostile to the younger, paving the way for their later rejection of Kullervo. When he is sold into slavery his older brother and sister both tell him – in long lines of verse – how much they won't miss him. His exile separates him both geographically and emotionally from his mother and sister, so that when he meets Wanōna again we can accept it as reasonable that he fails to recognize her.

Second, Kullervo's relationship with his sister. In *Kalevala* he has none, and because of the two-family combination he meets her for the first time on the occasion of the incest. Tolkien considerably expands and complicates this relationship, building up the childhood closeness of the twins and emphasizing their alienation from their older siblings and their consequent reliance on one another. Kullervo and Wanōna spend more time with each other than with anyone else. They are neglected 'wild' children who roam the woodlands, their only friend the hound Musti, a dog with supernatural powers who acts as both companion and protector. When Kullervo is sold into slavery by Untamo, he is followed by Musti, but cut off from his family. He declares that he will miss no one but Wanōna, yet in his exile he forgets her entirely, and fails to recognize her when by accident they meet again, with fatal consequences.

Third, Kullervo's personality and appearance. Again, in *Kalevala* there is none, or very little. His characteristics in the Finnish epic are precocious strength and an aptitude for magic. Barely three days old, he kicks his cradle to splinters. Set to rock an infant not long afterward, he breaks the baby's bones, gouges out his eyes, and burns his cradle. In addition, he is apparently indestructible, for Untamo has three tries at killing him, first by drowning, next by burning, and finally by hanging. Nothing works. He survives the drowning and 'measures the sea.' He escapes the burning and plays in the ashes. He is found on the hanging tree carving pictures in the bark. Set to clear a field he creates a wasteland; told to build a fence he makes an impenetrable enclosure with no way in or out; assigned to threshing grain he reduces it to dust. No reason or motive, except that he was rocked too hard as a baby, is given for this extreme behavior. It's just the way he is. You can't take him anywhere. Rather oddly, he is also handsome and a bit of a dandy, described as having 'finest locks of yellow colour', 'blue-dyed stockings', and 'shoes of best of leather.'

Tolkien's Kullervo is equally strong, but far from handsome or fashionable. He is 'swart' and 'ill-favoured and crooked', low in stature, and 'broad and ill knit and knotty and unrestrained and unsoftened.' Yet we come to understand him and even feel sympathy for him. The big difference between Tolkien's Kullervo and the one in *Kalevala* is that while their actions are the same (both do all the weird things I've described), Tolkien's Kullervo is clearly marked and motivated by early trauma. He is scarred by his father's murder and embittered by his and his mother's enslavement and cruel treatment by Untamo. He grows crooked for lack of a mother's care. Tolkien portrays him as sullen, resentful, angry, and alienated, close only to his sister Wanōna and the hound Musti. 'No tender feelings would he let his heart cherish for his folk afar.' He nurses grudges, he's lonely and a loner, a perpetual outsider, one of those people forever on the fringe of society unable or unwilling to fit in. Among Tolkien's many characters Kullervo stands out for his emotional and psychological complexity, exceeded only by an equivalent or greater complexity in his direct literary descendant, Túrin Turambar.

Fourth, his dog. There is no such supernatural animal as the great hound Musti in this part of *Kalevala*, though there is a black dog called Musti (which simply means 'Blackie' in Finnish) who after the second family has all died follows Kullervo into the forest to the place where he kills himself. In contrast, Tolkien's Musti is a significant character in the story, and plays an active part in several episodes. He initially belongs to Kalervo, and on the occasion of Untamo's raid, returns to the homestead to find it destroyed, his master killed and his wife, the lone survivor, captured. He follows her, but stays in the wild, where he becomes the friend and mentor of her two children Kullervo and Wanōna, and is associated with the dog of Tuoni, Lord of Death. Tolkien is tapping in to a standard mythological convention here, the connection between dogs and death and the underworld, which, although Musti is not the dog of Tuoni, nevertheless foreshadows by his presence the tragedy to come. While not of the underworld, Musti is described as 'a dog of fell might and strength and of great knowledge'. He is a shape-changer and a practitioner of magic which he passes on to Kullervo, instructing him in 'things darker and dimmer and farther back even . . . before their magic days'.

Musti becomes a kind of tutelary figure to Kullervo, and gives him magic talismans, three hairs from his coat with which to summon or invoke him in time of danger. These hairs save Kullervo from Untamo's three attempts to kill him, explicitly with the first (drowning), by implication in the second (burning), and again explicitly in the third (hanging), where the narrative is unequivocal that 'this magic that had saved Kullervo's life was the last hair of Musti'. Musti's magic is 'about' Kullervo from then on. Musti follows him when he is sold into slavery, and teaches him the magic that later enables him to use the wolves and bears to kill the smith's wife. In Tolkien's notes for the uncompleted ending of the story Musti reappears twice, once when he is killed in Kullervo's raid on Untamo's homestead, and at the scene of the suicide where Kullervo stumbles over the 'body of dead Musti'.

Fifth, his weapons. Like his *Kalevala* counterpart, Tolkien's Kullervo has both a knife and a sword. In *Kalevala* Kullervo laments the breaking of his knife, 'this iron ... heirloom from my father' (Runo XXXIII ll. 92–93), and explains to the smith's wife while she is being gnawed by bears and wolves that this is her punishment for causing him to break his knife. In Tolkien's story the knife has a greater history. It is given to the infant Kullervo when his mother first tells him of the Death of Kalervo (capitalized as if it were a story in itself). It is described as 'a great knife curiously wrought' that his mother had 'caught from the wall' when Untamo descended on the homestead, but had no chance to use, so swift was the attack. The knife has a name, Sikki, and is instrumental (together with the hair of Musti) in saving Kullervo from being hanged. It is this knife with which the boy carves pictures on the tree, wolves and bears and a huge hound, as well as great fish said to be 'Kalervo's sign of old'. The breaking of his knife on the stone in the cake causes Kullervo to lament its loss in verse, addressing the knife by name, calling it his only comrade and 'thou iron of Kalervo'. The sword makes its appearance late in the story, after Kullervo has met Wanōna again, and their tragedy has taken place. He takes the sword to kill Untamo, and makes it the willing instrument of his own death.

Sixth, the incest, which is the story's emotional climax. As noted above, in *Kalevala* this episode is a conflation of disparate *runos* from the far east of Finland, from Ingria, Karelia, and Archangel, and featuring different heroes with different names. Lönnrot smoothed the edges and regularized the hero's name to conform to the existing *runos* in his compilation. His Kullervo, on his way home after paying the taxes, accosts a succession of girls, inviting each into his sleigh. The third girl is the one who accepts, and theirs is a brief encounter quickly followed by the exchange of family information revealing the incest, and leading to her suicide. The scene is potentially tragic, but handled so quickly and tersely that it's over almost before you know it.

Tolkien makes much more of the event, and builds up to it carefully. His Kullervo, after his murder by proxy of the smith's wife, and while on the run and on his way to settle his score with Untamo, is met by the mysterious Lady of the Forest, who tells him the path he should follow and counsels him to avoid the wooded mountain, where 'ill will find him'. Of course he ignores her advice, and goes to 'drink the sunlight' on the mountain. Here, in a clearing on the mountain he sees a maiden who tells him she is 'lost in the evil woods'. At sight of her he forgets his quest, and asks her to be his 'comrade.' She is frightened, telling him that 'Death walketh with thee', and 'Little does thy look consort with maidens'. Angry that she has made fun of his ugliness and hurt that she has rejected him, he pursues her through the woods and carries her off. Though at first she rejects his advances, she does not long resist him, and they live together in apparent happiness in the wild until the fatal day when she asks him to tell her who his kinfolk are.

His reply that he is the son of Kalervo is the revelation

that leads to her realization that she and her lover are brother and sister. In Tolkien's treatment it becomes one of the most dramatic moments in the story, for Tolkien so manages the scene that the reader realizes the truth before Kullervo does. The maiden says no word of her discovery but stands gazing at him 'with outstretched hand', crying out that her path has led her 'deeper deeper into darkness/ Deeper deeper into sorrow/ Into woe and into horror. . . . For I go in dark and terror/ Down to Tuoni to the River.' Running away from Kullervo 'like a shivering ray of light in the dawn light' she comes to the waterfall and throws herself over the brink. But this is all we are told about her at this point. Though she recounts her own story, she does not reveal her parentage. Nor does Tolkien reveal it directly, letting her subsequent suicide and Kullervo's awakened memory, his 'old knowledge' of her speech and manner and the violence of her reaction underscore without explaining the tragedy of the situation. Only at the end of the story is Kullervo made to understand who she is and realize what he has done.

Seventh and last, the ending. Lönnrot's conflated and ill-assorted version takes Kullervo back to his second family, then to war against Untamo, then home to find that all his second family are now dead, and finally to his decision to end his life by asking his sword if it is willing to kill him. It is and it does and he dies, still alienated, isolated and alone. Tolkien left his version unfinished, breaking it off at the point where Kullervo, horrified in dawning suspicion of who the maiden is, and witness to her suicide, takes his sword and rushes blindly into the dark. But Tolkien had the end in mind, and a clear sense of how he wanted to treat it. Jotted outline notes have Kullervo go back to Untamo's home, kill him and lay it waste, then be visited in a dream by his mother's ghost who says that she has met her daughter in the underworld and confirms that she is the maiden who killed herself. It seems clear that Tolkien intended this to be the delayed moment of dyscatastrophe from which there is no upward turn, the hitherto-withheld information that he has violated his sister. Waking in terror from this overload of shame and sorrow, the anguished Kullervo rushes into the woods wailing 'Kivutar' (an alternate name for his sister), and comes to the glade where they first met. It is here that he asks his sword if it will kill him. It is more than willing, and he dies on its point.

Both Tolkien's re-working of his source and his story's relation to his subsequent work are clear. His Kullervo is the hinge between the rather weird Kullervo of *Kalevala* and the tragic, mixed-up Túrin Turambar of the 'Silmarillion', providing Túrin with all the family trauma, all the pent-up anger and resentment, all the negative emotions which fuel that character's bad decisions and make him so memorable. The geeky misfit of *Kalevala* becomes the angry, alienated, grudge-nursing outsider of *The Story of Kullervo*, who in turn develops into the fuller, more psychologically developed, self-isolating figure of Túrin Turambar, clearly related to his precursors but given a more coherent world and clearer framework within which to act out his tragedy.

Tolkien smooths *Kalevala*'s awkward two-family struc-
ture into one family with several siblings and this in turn
becomes the war-torn and disastrously reunited family of
Túrin. The unknown and unnamed sister of *Kalevala*
becomes Wanōna, 'Weeping', in *The Story of Kullervo*,
Kullervo's twin and companion in hardship, and Wanōna
in turn contributes to both Túrin's dearly loved and missed
sister Lalaith, 'Laughter', and to the never-seen Niënor
'Mourning', who becomes Níniel, the 'Tear-maiden' whom
he meets and marries, all-unknowing who she is. All these
meanings are significant, but the one for Wanōna is an
unmistakable precursor of the names for Túrin's never-
before-seen sister/wife. It is worth noting that in Tolkien's
outline for the story's ending, his Kullervo cries out to his
sister calling her *Kivutar*, 'Pain'. In *Kalevala* Kivutar is the
goddess of Pain and Suffering. While Edith was clearly
wife, not sister, their teenage romance and subsequent
enforced separation and what Tolkien called 'the dreadful
sufferings of our childhoods, from which we rescued one
another' (*Letters*, p. 421) are strong reminders of the loneliness of Kullervo and Wanōna as children, and of Kullervo's
anguish when she leaves him in death.

Kullervo's knife Sikki, all that he has of his father, finds
a prominent place in the *Unfinished Tales* version of the
'Narn i Hin Húrin', where 'curiously wrought' becomes
'Elf-wrought' and the knife, here not an heirloom but a
birthday present, is given to Túrin on his eighth birthday
by his father, who describes it as 'a bitter blade' (*Unfinished
Tales*, p. 64). Túrin gives the knife to the serving-man,

Sador, but later misses it and mourns its loss. It seems clear, however, that the knife is a tool rather than a weapon, unlike the grim and foreboding sword which becomes Kullervo's death, or the one whose multiple identities, first as Anglachel then Gurthang, then Mormegil, give Túrin an equal identity and a name, and eventually take his life. However, as Richard West has pointed out, Tolkien developed the weapon 'far beyond what he found in his Finnish source', making it 'an embodiment of the ill fate that besets the hero' (*Tolkien's Legendarium*, p. 239).

Since the sword is the efficient cause of the hero's death, it is worth comparing the three instances, first in *Kalevala*, then in *The Story of Kullervo*, last in the story of Túrin, which distinguish it from other swords belonging to other Tolkien heroes: the fact that it speaks and interacts with the hero. Here is the speech in *Kalevala*:

> Wherefore at thy heart's desire
> Should I not thy flesh devour,
> And drink up they blood so evil?
> I who guiltless flesh have eaten,
> Drank the blood of those who sinned not?

Here is *The Story of Kullervo* version that appears in Tolkien's plot notes:

> The sword says if it had joy in the death of Untamo how much in death of even wickeder Kullervo. And it had slaid [*sic*] many an innocent person, even his mother, so it would not boggle over K.

And here is the sword to Túrin in the version in *The Silmarillion*:

> Yea, I will drink thy blood gladly, that so I may forget the blood of Beleg my master, and the blood of Brandir slain unjustly. I will slay thee swiftly. (*The Silmarillion*, p. 225)

While there is not a great deal of difference among the three versions (though the second is reportage rather than direct speech), the last two are closer to one another than either is to the first. In place of the more general 'guiltless flesh' and 'those who sinned not' of the primary *Kalevala* source, the other two passages cite specific names of people whom the sword has killed, in Tolkien's note associating wicked Untamo with wickeder Kullervo, and in *The Silmarillion* contrasting guilty Túrin with innocent Beleg and Brandir. Both of Tolkien's swords are more judgmental, have more knowledge, more personality, and more dramatic impact than their *Kalevala* model. It is worth noting that in his essay 'On "The Kalevala"' Tolkien described the voice of Kullervo's sword as that of 'a cruel and cynical ruffian,' foreshadowing the darker aspects he later gave to his own sword Anglachel in the story of Túrin.

An unexpected carry-over from this early story to the 'Silmarillion' material is the episode of Kullervo's return, crying aloud his sister's name, to the waterfall where she killed herself. It reappears in 'Of Tuor and his Coming to Gondolin' in *Unfinished Tales*, where it becomes a vivid, briefly-flashed moment in which Tuor and Voronwë at the Falls of Ivrin hear 'a cry in the woods' and glimpse 'a

tall Man, armed, clad in black, with a long sword drawn'
crying aloud in grief the name, 'Ivrin, Faelivrin!' Minimal
explanation is given. 'They knew not,' says the narrative,
'that ... this was Túrin son of Húrin' and never again 'did
the paths of those kinsmen [Tuor and Túrin] ... draw
together' (*Unfinished Tales*, pp. 37–8). Curiously, Túrin's
anguish and loss is not for his sister/wife Níniel, as we
might expect, but for Finduilas, the elf-maiden who loves
him and for whose death he is somehow responsible.
The intrusion of this moment into 'The Story of Tuor'
is a clear borrowing from Tolkien's note outline where
Kullervo, returning to the falls where she has killed herself,
cries aloud for 'Kivutar'. In 'The Story of Tuor' it is grief
witnessed from the outside by an audience ignorant of the
circumstances and thus unable to comprehend the anguish
and loss. The scene is disturbing, intentionally dislocated,
an interlace gesture from one story to another. The fact
that both stories gesture toward the even earlier story is
eloquent testimony to the hold that Tolkien's Kullervo had
on his imagination.

The most surprising revelation is that Huan the
Hound, the supernatural helper of Beren and Lúthien, did
not spring fully formed from Tolkien's brow, but has a
clear forerunner in Musti. Musti is perhaps Tolkien's most
noteworthy addition to his *Kalevala* source, and Huan is,
after Túrin himself, the clearest avatar carried over from
the earlier story to the world of the legendarium. Talking
(and helping) animals are not unknown in the world of
Middle-earth. The fox (though he is an anomaly) in Book

One of *The Fellowship of the Ring*, the talking thrush, and the raven Roäc son of Carc in *The Hobbit*, the eagles in both *The Hobbit* and *The Lord of the Rings* and the dog Garm from *Farmer Giles* are the best examples; that is unless you count talking dragons such as Smaug and Glaurung, who have solid precursors. Glaurung is plainly derived from the Fáfnir of the *Poetic Edda*, where Smaug and *Farmer Giles*'s Chrysophylax are comic examples, nearer in type to Kenneth Grahame's Reluctant Dragon than to Icelandic mythology, and Garm belongs in that same parodic category.

Musti is a bit different; he is Tolkien's best example of a particular fairy-tale archetype, the animal helper; a type that includes Puss-in-Boots, the talking horse Falada of the Grimms' 'The Goose-girl', the Firebird in the story of Prince Ivan, The Little Humpbacked Horse, and various shape-changing bears and wolves in Norse and Icelandic folktales. In Tolkien's own work, Beorn of *The Hobbit* comes close, but he is nearer in type to the shape-changers of the sagas than to the animals of fairy-tale, and his own animals, though they walk on their hind legs and wait table, are not magical helpers but mere circus performers. Huan is a far better representative of the archetype. Nevertheless, he does not derive immediately from his fairy-tale predecessors but is in direct descent from Musti, whose obvious inheritor he is. In both stories the loyal, supernatural hound is a powerful character in his own right, and in both stories the hound is a victim of his own loyalty, following the hero to his death in a climactic and violent episode late in the narrative.

The Story of Kullervo, then, was the fuse that 'set the rocket off in story' (*Letters*, p. 214) as Tolkien wrote to Auden. He was not exaggerating. This very early narrative, incomplete and derivative as it is, ignited his imagination and was his earliest prefigurement of some of the most memorable literary figures and moments in the 'Silmarillion'. Moreover, it is not beyond conjecture that without the former, we might not have the latter, at least not in the form in which we know it. The hapless orphan, the unknown sister, the heirloom knife, the broken family and its psychological results, the forbidden love between lonely young people, the despair and self-destruction on the point of a sword, all transfer into 'The Tale of the Children of Húrin', not direct from *Kalevala* but filtered through *The Story of Kullervo*. We can now see where these elements came from, and how they got to be what they are. Most telling, paradoxically because perhaps least necessary, is the move from Musti to Huan – a figure almost unchanged save for his name. It seems clear that Tolkien found Musti simply too good to waste, and recycled him from the unfinished early story to the later and more fully realized fairytale context of the romance of Beren and Lúthien.

The Story of Kullervo was Tolkien's earliest attempt at retelling – and in the process 'reorganizing' – an already-existing tale. As such, it occupies an important place in his canon. Furthermore, it is a significant step on the winding road from imitation to invention, a trial piece by the orphan boy, university undergraduate, returning soldier who loved *Kalevala*, resonated with Kullervo, and felt the lack of 'something of the same sort that belonged to the English'.

VERLYN FLIEGER

BIBLIOGRAPHY

Carpenter, Humphrey. *J.R.R. Tolkien: a biography*. London: George Allen & Unwin, 1977.

Comparetti, Domenico. *The Traditional Poetry of the Finns*, trans. Isabela M. Anderton. London: Longmans, Green, and Co., 1898.

Dorson, Richard M. *The British Folklorists: A History*. Chicago: University of Chicago Press, 1968.

Finnish Folk Poetry Epic, Edited and Translated Matti Kuusi, Keith Bosley, and Michael Branch. Helsinki: Finnish Literature Society, 1977.

Garth, John. '"The road from adaptation to invention": How Tolkien Came to the Brink of Middle-earth in 1914,' *Tolkien Studies* XI. Morgantown West Virginia: West Virginia University Press, 2014.

'Hausa Folktales' by F.W.H.M. in *African Affairs*, Oxford University Press, 1914; XIII 457.

Helms, Randel. *Tolkien and the Silmarils*. Boston: Houghton Mifflin Company, 1981.

Higgins, Andrew. 'The Genesis of J.R.R. Tolkien's Mythology.'

Thesis in fulfillment of PhD, Cardiff Metropolitan University, 2015.

Lang, Andrew. *Custom and Myth*, 2nd edition. London: Longmans, Green, and Co., 1893.

Lönnrot, Elias. *Kalevala*, 2 vols. Translated W.F. Kirby. London: Dent, Everyman's Library, 1907.

——. *Kalevala: Epic of the Finnish* People, 2nd edition. Translated Eino Friberg. Helsinki: Otava Publishing Company, Ltd., 1988.

——. *The Kalevala: Or Poems of the Kaleva District*. Translated Francis Magoun. Cambridge: Harvard University Press, 1963.

Noad, Charles. E. 'On the Construction of "The Silmarillion"' in *Tolkien's Legendarium: Essays on* The History of Middle-earth, ed. Verlyn Flieger and Carl F. Hostetter. Westport, Connecticut: Greenwood Press, 2000.

Pentikainen, Juha. *Kalevala Mythology*, Translated and edited Ritva Poom. Bloomington: Indiana University Press, 1987.

Petty, Anne. C. 'Identifying England's Lönnrot' in *Tolkien Studies*, Vol. I. Morgantown: West Virginia University Press, 2004.

Scull, Christina and Wayne G. Hammond. *The J.R.R. Tolkien Companion and Guide: Chronology* and *Reader's Guide*. London: HarperCollins*Publishers*, 2006.

Shippey, Tom. *The Road to Middle-earth*. Revised and expanded ed. London: HarperCollins*Publishers*, 2005.

Swank, Kris. 'The Irish Otherworld Voyage of Roverandom,' in *Tolkien Studies* Volume XII. Morgantown, West Virginia University Press, 2015.

Tolkien, J.R.R. *Beowulf and the Critics*, Edited Michael D.C. Drout. Tempe, AZ. Arizona Center for Medieval and Renaissance Studies, 2002.

——. *The Book of Lost Tales, Part One*. Boston: Houghton Mifflin Company, 1983.

——. *The Letters of J.R.R. Tolkien*, ed. Humphrey Carpenter. London: George Allen & Unwin, 1981.

——. *The Lord of the Rings*. London: HarperCollins*Publishers*, 1991.

——. 'The Etymologies', *The Lost Road*, ed. Christopher Tolkien. London: Unwin Hyman, 1987.

——. *Qenyaqetsa: The Qenya Phonology and Lexicon*, Edited Christopher Gilson, Carl F. Hostetter, Patrick Wynne and Arden R. Smith. *Parma Eldalamberon* 12. Cupertino, CA, 1998.

——. 'The Shores of Faëry', *The Book of Lost Tales, Part Two*, ed. Christopher Tolkien. London: George Allen & Unwin, 1984.

——. *The Silmarillion*, 2nd edition, ed. Christopher Tolkien. London: HarperCollins *Publishers*, 1999.

——. 'The Story of Kullervo' edited and transcribed Verlyn Flieger. *Tolkien Studies*, Vol. VII, Morgantown: West Virginia University Press, 2010.

——. *Tolkien On Fairy-stories*. Expanded edition, with commentary and notes. Edited Verlyn Flieger and Douglas A. Anderson. London: HarperCollins*Publishers*, 2008.

——. 'The Voyage of Éarendel the Evening Star', *The Book of Lost Tales, Part Two*, ed. Christopher Tolkien. London: George Allen & Unwin, 1984.

Tremearne, Major Arthur John Newman. *Hausa Folktales.* London: J. Bale, Sons & Danielson, 1914.

West, Richard. C. 'Setting the Rocket off in Story', *Tolkien and the Invention of Myth*, ed. Jane Chance. Lexington, KY: The University Press of Kentucky, 2004.

——. 'Túrin's *Ofermod*' in *Tolkien's Legendarium: Essays on The History of Middle-earth*, ed. Verlyn Flieger and Carl F. Hostetter. Westport, Connecticut: Greenwood Press, 2000.